The Poetic Whore

FLENARDO

Publisher's Note: This is a work of fiction. Names, characters, places and incidents are products of the author's imagination. Locale and public names are sometimes used for atmospheric purposes. Any resemblance to actual people, living or dead, or to businesses, companies, events or institutions are completely coincidental.

Published by
Flenardo Taylor Publishing

Revised by Marsha Dickson

ISBN: 978-0615944593

DEDICATION

I dedicate this book to the memory of my Mom, who passed away without having the chance to watch me perform poetry on the stage. As a final honor, I wrote an entire book so the world can see your son as you created him to be. I love you, Mary Emma Taylor.

Books by Flenardo

CHAPTER 1
MALAKAI

I can't believe this bitch got me in one of those crazy-ass scams again! She is out here blackmailing a preacher who couldn't keep his dick in his damn pants. So, while he's out there preaching about Moses parting the Red Sea, I've got Asperilla's pussy parted and this tongue is the staff, so you know I am about to eat the fuck out of this pussy.

I must admit, this shit is so damn good. I'm praying to God that He doesn't punish me too hard for fucking in His house. All you hear is moans and groans as I slide this thick tongue in and out of her ass.

"Eat this chocha, my black Mandingo," she proclaimed.

For some odd reason, that shit turns me on as I pick her up by the waist and start to rodeo her pussy into my mouth. She likes it rough with her freaky ass. I pick her up and flip her ass upside down so her legs are on my shoulders and her mouth on my dick. This is our version of the Statue of Liberty: mouth, balls, and all. Damn, I love this freak.

We are gulping and slurping each other dry, 'til sweat is pouring out of us. I can hear the church members clapping and praising, as I lay her back down on the desk. She always had this thing she does before I give her the dick; she sucks her fingers and then she plays with her cat 'til it gushes sweet juices everywhere. I am so damn rock hard that I jump in the pussy, fucking her like a jack rabbit because she loves it. I grabbed her by the throat.

"Beat this pussy up, Malakai!" she yells.

We don't realize that the pastor has an intercom in his office that's connected to the sanctuary. We accidently knock that bitch on, and our fuck session is now being broadcast to everyone in the pews.

"Bitch, take this dick," I groan. "Every damn inch and love it, you filthy dog."

She's throwing the pussy back. "Is that all you got, Papi? Fuck this pussy 'til it bleeds!"

I start to beat it like a locomotive at full speed ahead, sticking her pussy like I'm shanking a person's heart. She cums all down my legs, and right before I unleash my load, the pastor's door flies open.

"What the fuck is this? I mean, my God, what are you doing?" he says as he turns the intercom off.

Asperilla slides off my dick. "Pastor Johnson don't be all surprised. You owe my bitches money, and you thought you could fuck and run. Well, I'm here to collect."

I know he's about to say something stupid as I'm standing here naked with my dick in my hand.

"I don't-,"

Before he finishes the sentence, I walk over and slap the shit out of his ass. "Pastor, you're fucking with my money. You better get that shit out of the damn tithes and offering."

2

"Please," he says, "my congregation is outside. Can we please talk about this another time?"

"Look, Pastor," I say, "I've never killed a man of God, but we will remix Cain and Abel in this muthafucka if you say something else wrong out of your damn mouth."

I finally pull my pants up, dick still rock hard. This bitch is going to pay extra for fucking up my nut. Asperilla has a sick smile on her face, with her nasty ass; she must have read my mind, because she gets on her knees and starts sucking me off through the zipper.

"Take notes, Pastor. This is business and pleasure. Where is my damn money?" I grab my 9mm from the holster, cock it and point it at his head.

"Okay," he says, finally giving in, "there is no need for anyone to die today, especially in the church."

"Well, at least you won't have far to go for a funeral," I laugh. He goes to his safe and starts to count my money. I keep my 9mm aimed right at his ass while Asperilla sucks the skin off my dick. I can feel my last vein pop up as she grabs my ass and makes me force-feed her this nut. She swallows and gets up.

"I love you, Papi," she says with a smile.

"Hurry up" I demand as I zip my pants and snatch $10,000 from his hand.

He paid $5,000 for last weekend's thrill with the three girls, since Asperilla busted in their room and took pictures; he was more than willing to pay the price.

"Can you all please give me the pictures before you go out the back door," Pastor Johnson pleads, "so I can try to clean up the mess ya'll made in my church? Every member in my church heard you all humping and groaning on the intercom. I know I have done some low-down shit as a pastor, but to have sex in God's house is beyond insane. You got your money, and I got my pictures, so please, just go."

Asperilla smiles. "Pastor, next time, I'll charge you double, and don't think about calling the police. We'd hate to kidnap your wife, drug her, and then pimp her out. Imagine that Malakai... First Lady of Mount Liberty; we could make a fortune off her ass. You know how many people in the streets fantasize about fucking a preacher's wife?"

"It sounds good, baby, but I have had my share of church for today."

We get our things and head out the back door. I have no idea how I became this coldhearted person. I once was a kid that grew up in church, girls would pass me by because my clothing wasn't tight, I had no ride, and I couldn't hold a nut long enough, even if someone had a gun pointed at my head.

My, my, my, times have changed.

"Pleasure is a bitch," I say to the pastor as we walk out the door. "You better stay with your wife, because next time you might not be so lucky."

CHAPTER 2
PASTOR JOHNSON

Those nasty freaks had the audacity to run up in my church this morning. I'm going to look like a born-again fool out there; trying to explain to the members about the sex session they heard on the intercom. As soon as I reach the pulpit, I hear the commotion in the pews, and the look on my wife's face spells guilty. I did what any other preacher would do at a time like this. I just started praying aloud.

"Father God, I ask now that You please come down and restore order into Your house. I ask that You touch every heart today and give me wisdom on the things I am about to say. I pray that You prevent any rumors and lies that will come from the mouth of deceivers and manipulators. God, we all have sinned and come short of Your glory, but we do know right from wrong. Father God, You are the true and living God, and I ask that You heal the tormented souls of the two people that are possessed with the sex demon! I thank You for strength, because this morning, I walked through the valley of the shadow of death, and I feared no evil! With the right hand on your Word, I begin to lay hands and protect Your house from the evildoers. Father God, I thank You for protecting this flock, and please keep a watch out for us every step of the way; it is in Your precious and everlasting Son's name we pray. Amen!"

After the prayer, I hear a few members shouting and catching the spirit while a few of the older folks walk out. I knew this drama would have an effect on me and my family. If I dismiss church, I would be going out like a coward, so I ask the choir to sing before the sermon. One thing about this smooth pastor is that I can bring the Word.

I preach until my robe is filled with sweat, and even though a few souls were saved, I know mine is in danger of being exposed.

After the service, I shook the hands of my congregation members and thanked them for coming and praising with us today. I pull off my messy situation like Lebron James in game six of the NBA finals.

I go to my office after seeing everyone off and the deacons are standing at my office door.

Deacon Willis angrily speaks, "I am very unhappy about this morning's disturbance. Your father would be turning over in his grave if he knew of this nonsense."

I glance at the other deacons and say, "Is there anyone else who would like to express himself."

Once again, I'm quick on my feet gossiping, "There is a new sex craze sweeping the city and there is a cult that loves to have sex in public."

A few members begin to say, "Yeah, I heard of that group; I think a few of them were caught having sex at the park."

I knew they were lying because I was making this crap up with a straight face. It was a beautiful lie, but after I pull off the impossible, I will be clear of this in a few weeks.

Deacon Willis extends his hand in his sympathetic voice, "Pastor, I have no idea what's happening in the city. I am too old to be keeping up with this new generation's nastiness."

We shake hands.

They leave my office, and I go through my cell, looking for someone to clean up this morning's bullshit. If I could use that sexy Olivia character off the hit show Scandal, best believe I would hire her, regardless of the price.

I called my lawyer instead and explained to him what happened in church. I disclosed to him about the sex crazed rumor that I told the deacons.

"Look, I need your help spreading this rumor throughout the city," I announced.

He tells me, "this isn't the first time that people were caught or heard of having sex in God's house. Calm down. I know a few friends down at the local news station, and they would love to sell your wild story to the public."

"Nothing is free in this world, so I would make sure that you get extra money for this cover up," I acknowledge.

I also call Jerrod, my homeboy since high school, who would steal and kill if the cash was right.

We ran the streets together for years but all of that changed when I decided to become a pastor.

I grew up showing respect for my dad. Besides, I was a Preacher's Kid. Even in my youth, I was very sneaky, and I learned that being a PK had its advantages. I did some wild things, and when I did get caught, my father always kept a ram in the bush to ensure my nose was clean. I smile as I reminisce about the beautiful days as a teenager.

I come out of the twilight zone as Jerrod answers my call. "Carlos, Carlos,'' he says to get my attention.

"Jerrod," I say as I'm brought back to reality, "it's been a minute. How are you?"

"Man, you know me," he says, "one day at a time."

"Jerrod," I cut him off before he could start rambling about our last sexcapade. "I need a favor. Meet me at the church tomorrow evening. I have a situation for you to handle.

"But Jerrod, pay attention. This is important. I'm caught up in some bullshit, and I need you to help clear my name just in case something happens. I had sex with three ladies last week, and the pictures are being leaked. So, you have to shakedown one of the escorts."

Jerrod excitedly says, "Man, I am ready for some action. It's been a while since I had a little fun."

"I will see you around six tomorrow night. I can't thank you enough."

"You know I am the best person for the job. I'll be there," he says with a laugh.

As soon as I hang up the phone, my beautiful wife comes into the office with tears running down her face.

"Carlos, I am so tired of your drama. I refuse to be the good wife, the perfect First Lady, while you are a whoremonger. God doesn't like ugly and one day, He will tear down your world."

I know she has a point, but I will never confess to anything. God will know, but I'll take the rest of my lies to my grave. I grab her hand and attempt to explain that I'm innocent.

"I have been faithful since our last therapy session," I say.

She snatches her hand back. "I will see you at home, if you remember the address."

Tasha leaves with tears still wet on her face.

I know she is upset, so after I finish plotting my revenge, I'll take my wife out for a lovely night on the town.

I also know God is watching me, so I will go ahead and change my ways after my next massage appointment.

I dial my wife's cell, "Tasha, please meet me downtown at our favorite restaurant at 6pm, so we can enjoy a beautiful evening together."

She speaks with no hesitation, "Sure, baby. I would love to."

Carlos thinks to himself, that response was too damn quick, but I will make it up to her later on tonight.

You would think that after the pregnancy scare, I would have learned my lesson, but some dogs only change when they're neutered.

I bump right into Brandi Sykes, the Choir Director, as I am heading to the pulpit to retrieve my Bible.

She smiles, "You are a compulsive liar, and you can try to cover up the drama of this morning, but I can always see through your wolf skin. You should have stayed with me; at least I knew how to keep my mouth shut."

"For Pete's sake, you are Tasha's friend. I have no time for this foolishness," I tell her. "Our business arrangement ended the day you thought you should be the First Lady. Besides, I don't backtrack, and I'm turning over a new leaf. There will be changes coming to Mt. Liberty."

CHAPTER 3
MALAKAI

We travel down I-275 in my candy red Ferrari Enzo. It feels so damn good to know I'm the only nigga in the state of Florida with this ride. We're laughing from the episode at the church. Asperilla is one of those bitches that will do anything for her man, but she will also do anything for cash. Cash comes first. Music is blasting as we move down the road, and the wind is feeling good on a man's soul.

I have a busy night ahead of me. I have to hustle up my side business and continue promoting my club. I have the hottest spot in Tampa, one in Cali, and two in New York. Not bad for a poet that everyone passed up ten years ago.

I'm meeting some old friends from Cuba at International Mall, but first I need to drop Asperilla off at the house.

She'll probably go to sleep. She could have her own mother murdered then go home and sleep it off like it was a headache or something. One word: Ruthless!

We pulled up to my house on the waterfront. I love this house. I even have a boat tied to the dock, and I can't even sail. But I've got money, so I bought it. We go into the house so I can jump in the shower before I ride back out. Asperilla wants to sneak a quickie in, so I have to bang her head against the shower door real quick. I guess that's her way of saying, "Have fun this evening."

--------------------᧞᧞᧞᧞᧞᧞----------------------

As I'm walking down the stairs, I receive a text message confirming that they want to make another transaction. I know what y'all are thinking, this dude is pushing drugs. Hell nah, I push pussy, because that's the only thing in business since the world has been spinning.

I am a club owner and poet by day, and I run one of the best escort services in the United States by night.

I headed out to the mall. I can do this city; it's good to me. I started out with nothing, but now everyone knows my name.

It doesn't take long for Edmundo to find me in the crowded store. This dude always travels with an entourage. We became friends when I met him as an up-and-coming poet, and his damn girl wanted to meet me.

Since that day, he's always said, "If a man can pull my woman without money, then I know he's the dude I want on my team."

Edmundo is the type of man that can make a lady's heart melt. He has the Cuban look that make Adam Rodriguez seems like shit. Underneath those looks, he has the mind of a killer.

One time, I was at his spot, and he was upstairs fucking this woman. Next thing I know, he's dragging her ass downstairs by her hair. He went into a secret room with a shark tank and threw her ass in it. I was shocked but played it cool. I asked Edmundo, "What the hell did she do to deserve that?" He said, "That bitch was talking like her pussy walks on water. I lost ten minutes of my life trying to get in that tight shit. Man, she wasted my time and a damn nut. I must admit, she was fine, but if you going to brag on yourself, you better walk the walk or walk the plank." Then he laughed and was like Nino off the movie New Jack City. "Cancel that bitch, I'll buy another one." I knew from that day forward to always have my shit on point when I deal with this dude.

I embraced my long-time buddy and we decided to go to a restaurant to talk.

I already know what he needs. He's looking for some of my girls to do a show tonight. One thing about me, I love my girls and will die for them. I never make them do this against their will. I respect my ladies, and they always keep me lavished in the finest things.

"Man," Edmundo says, "I need two Asians and one Russian off the menu."

"Dude, you're ordering them like they're drinks from a bar."

The whole table falls out laughing. We order our drinks and enjoy our meals.

He pulls me to the side and asks, "Do you have some ladies that are willing to travel to Cuba for a week or two?"

I tell him," I'll get back with you on that one."

Deep down, I just can't shake the shark incident. I know my ladies are the truth, but this man is really sick in the head at times. He always keeps his money long, but I have more. I could easily turn his ass down without even thinking twice about it.

I gave him a pound and told him he can pick his ladies up at the spot tonight. We exchange hugs and leave the scene.

Tonight is going to be one of those wild nights.

Just as I'm about to get into my ride, my phone rings. It's my co-owner at the club asking, "Are you going to perform tonight?"

I tell him, "I will get back to you on that one."

"The ladies are willing to pay double to have you feature tonight," he says.

"It's been a minute since this tongue unwinded. I'll turn it out, just have my music and band ready."

"Hell yeah," he says. "We are about to shut the city down. The one and only Malakai is about to get on the mic and make these freaks' panties wet." We both laugh.

"I have to make a run," I say, "but I'll get with you on the details. Don't tell anyone I'm performing, and we'll really blow their minds."

We ended the call, and I hopped in the car to head home. I'll prepare to unleash the poetic beast in me. Damn, it'll feel good to be in front of the crowd again.

Once again, I'm in my ride, heading to the house. I better go ahead and beat this nut out of me while I'm speeding down the highway. I got a feeling Asperilla will be walking through the house naked. She never gets tired of fucking.

I switch music and find me a song to beat this dick off to. Yeah, this will work. Fergalicious is on the radio. I can hit it slow and smooth off this, and then slang my nut out on the highway.

I pull up in my driveway, enter my home, and call for Asperilla. She's upstairs playing in the hot tub. She does look sexy with her smooth skin, long black hair, and those killer legs leading to the perfect ass and tits. I've always been in love with her, but tonight, there's something that I love just as much as Asperilla. My wife, Poetry; Spoken Word always makes my dick hard.

I tell Asperilla that I'll be going down to Poetic Heaven to perform tonight, and she's welcome to come if she likes.

She slowly stands up in the water and whispers, "I am always ready to cum."

"Well, please save it for tonight and I'll give you everything your soul needs," I expressed.

She laughs. "I know you will, or I will cut that thang off."

I'm not sure if I should laugh or take this woman seriously. I shrug it off.

Tonight, I'm gonna mix business with pleasure once again. I have to get the ladies ready for Edmundo and figure out how I'll seduce the crowd to make every woman's cunt drip while collecting my money at the same time.

"WHO NEEDS A STICK SHIFT WHEN YOU CAN
BEAT YOUR STICK AND SHIFT POEMS INSIDE OF
YOUR HEAD."

CHAPTER 4
MALAKAI

We pull up to *Poetic Heaven*, and the crowd is thick. I go in through the back door because I'm about to make a 'poetic entrance' like none other. I can hear the live band doing their thing, and the dude is killing it on the horn. It's going to be an explosive night. I hear the band saying they're about to take a break and will return for another set later. The DJ starts to spin the song, *Love Calls* by Kem. I can feel the crowd get into the groove.

I dip under the stage where we have a trap door. From here, I'll be lifted up before my performance. I'm all set. This will be mind-blowing. I have this bad woman named Sparkle down here with me, and we'll make this a night to remember.

I hear the DJ pump up the crowd.

"Tonight, the legend has returned. Ladies, I pray you all brought an extra pair of panties." He switches to my favorite theme song, Jodeci's *Freak 'N You.*

I rise from under the stage with my shirt off, in just my jeans and boots. Sparkle is on her knees and the smokescreen gives the impression that we're floating on air. The song has every woman grinding and licking their lips. Sparkle is bouncing up and down on my leg and hip.

The music stops, and the woman drops it down real slow and stops at the zipper of my pants. She slowly unbuttons my pants and reaches her hand in there. I stop and throw my head back like I'm about to get a hand job.

The crowd goes crazy when she slowly pulls out my mic.

She licks the tip of the mic, slowly rises to her feet, and gives it to me. She walks off the stage, throwing that ass all over the place in that hip hugging dress. The crowd goes into a frenzy.

I don't want to waste another second. I start on the crowd's favorite piece, *Candylicker*!

Sometimes I wonder if I am a fiend.
Because I have a passion to lick deep strokes
Like a little kid licking ice cream.
Oh yeah, best believe she is going to scream.
My tongue is like an automatic whipping machine,
That will have you wet before you even start to dream.
See, this freak will go to the extreme,
And my tongue is trained,
So, I'll never sink as I swim downstream.
See, I like to part a woman open
Like Moses did the Red Sea,
Tasting sweetness of honey
Every time I penetrate her peach tree.
Sucking juices like a bee does nectar from a flower.
I'm determined to devour all of her world power,
Leaving her with vibes and feelings
She can't even experience during a free happy hour.
I'll have her whole body motionless
Like the Eiffel Tower,

Delivering nothing but sexual pleasures

As I ring her bell for hours.

See, let me break down the word lick,

So, you can understand why I am a true Candylicker.

In boxing, the word lick means a blow with the fist,

I'll be delivering TKOs.

Every time I do figure eights with a twist of a kiss.

Yes, the word lick is a verb

That can leave you with something to say,

But you can't remember the words.

The word lick means to find the solution or

Understand the meaning.

See, I want to have her leaning.

All kinds of ways

While she experiences this sexual cleaning.

I want to slowly suck and lick the center

Of your Tootsie Pop,

As I send shockwaves through your soul

While you beg me not to stop.

Go ahead, grab the back of my head

And push it in real deep.

I promised that throughout the week,

Your knees will buckle

Every time you think about this freak.

I got that ancient Greek technique,

Like that god, Zeus,

Swirling and curling designs all over you

That will make you release your juice.

I'll be like Dora the Explorer,

All over your clitoral,

Sipping on your outer and inner lips

Before I even start to dip.

The sheets you would start to grip

As I circle roundtrips through your treasure ship.

Go ahead, get on top and twirl those hips

As my tongue cling to your hood

Like paper to a gem clip.

If this was Fast and the Furious,

I want you to ride my face

Like your soul was filled with nitrogen.

Hell, you can take me under,

And you still won't be able to cut off my oxygen.

I want you to imagine your climax being the finish line

While you whine, and I continue to dine.

If I haven't blew your mind, then I need to resign.

But I can see your body having

Convulsions and contractions,

So, I know you are pleased by my action.

Don't be afraid; go ahead, tell me you're cumming

While my tongue is a constant flicker.

See, I'm just a country brother,

And I just drain the hell out of that city slicker,

Having her hung over like hard liquor,
Swallowed whole by the Candylicker.

As I finish the piece, the ladies are taking off their panties, and throwing them on stage. One of them throws some edible panties my way. Of course, I pick them up and start to chew on them.

I tell the crowd, thanks for the love, and that I'll return again real soon.

Tonight was a great feeling for me. Returning to the mic made me think about the old days, when me and poetry were struggling to show the world that we were about to take over the planet.

I go backstage, change clothes, and prepare to meet Edmundo to deliver the ladies to him. I go to the VIP area where Asperilla and the ladies are waiting on me. Edmundo tells his people this is how we met, and everyone's telling me I killed that shit tonight.

I'm always humble when it comes to being a poet, so I say thanks and prepare to jump out of the poet role and into the businessman. I tell Edmundo that these ladies are the best on the planet.

"Man, you always know how to pick them," he says with a smile.

I give him the rundown on the girls, and he's delighted. Payment is taken care of through the secret accounts I have set up for transfers and deposits. I always conduct my business with caution.

Tonight is going to end on a high note. Edmundo gets the ladies he needs, and Asperilla is smiling, because she knows she's getting some good dick tonight.

I mingle with the crowd and thank everyone for coming out.

Poetic Heaven is still jumping off, and I enjoy the night.

When it's time for me'and Asperilla to head home, I have my pedal to the floor. I can't wait to get her out of that dress and eat that pussy. That's the only thing that's on my mind as I race down the highway.

CHAPTER 5
JERROD

Carlos is always running late. He's got me sitting here in this empty-ass parking lot. I barely come to church. I consider myself one of those CME goers: Christmas, Mother's Day, and Easter. Even then, I'm hunting for presents, single mothers, and whatever eggs I can crack. I would listen to some music, but I'm trying not to cause a scene in this neighborhood.

Carlos finally pulls up and walks over to the car.

I step out of my ride. "Bout time, man." I usually try to hold my cussing in front of this dude, but he is nowhere close to being a saint. I know it must be the money that keeps Tasha from leaving his trifling ass.

Carlos unlocks the church door as I follow closely behind him. We head to his office, and I ask him why he is always late for every meeting.

"Look Man, I was late because I was arguing with my wife about yesterday's church service," he says. "But enough beating around the bush. I'm caught up in a little situation, and I need you to bail me out."

Here we go again, Jerrod to the rescue. "Carlos, you really need to be careful where you plant those nasty seeds."

"Oh, you ready to become a preacher?" he shoots back.

"Not after watching you," I say. "I'd rather take my chances as a sinner."

He confesses with head bowed, "I was having sex with three ladies when another woman walks in the room and starts snapping pictures. They are using the photos to blackmail me and will reveal them to the church."

I hear the story he is telling me, and the only thing I can think about is this lucky bastard having three hoes in one night. I am not a bad looking dude, but I haven't had that experience yet.

"Carlos, was the pussy good? Was your face buried between their legs, or were you beating it like a real man when she started to take the pics?" I question. "Because it would be fucked up if the pictures are leaked and the church sees you being spanked with whips and getting dildos stuffed up your ass." I say, laughing, because I thought that picture would be hilarious.

"This is no joking matter," he says. "I need your help, Jerrod. I promise to do better with my extramarital affairs, and this is the last time I'll get trapped in the closet. I just need you to clear this one up for me. I know my wife will leave me for sure this time, and I will lose my church, as well. I have worked too hard to get on this level, and I ain't going out like Samson and losing my eyes over some tail!"

"Calm down, Carlos. You're worrying about the church and your wife, but what about me? I was the one that had to take care of your pregnant mistress. Yeah, you know, Pastor Allen's daughter, the one you were fucking after you met her during the revival! I was the one that took her to the abortion clinic two months later so you could preach the next Sunday without any worries! I keep a lot of dark secrets for you, but after this, you are responsible for your own problems!"

He got real quiet.

"You're right," he finally responds, "and I owe you a great deal of respect." He knows I have been his ace of spade since high school. We exchange pounds, and he apologizes.

I'm shocked. Carlos Johnson never tells anyone that he is sorry.

I feel bad for my old friend, and even though I am tired of his crazy ways, I am willing to bail him out again.

"Carlos, what do you need me to do this time?"

He plots and responds, "I want you to scare an escort name Cherry so bad until she shits her pants and give up every photo that was taken of me."

"Carlos, are you even sure this chick has the pictures?"

He says he's dead sure, but something is really fishy about this story. I know Carlos can be vindictive, so I need to give him the third degree before I cosign to something that could put me behind prison bars.

"Let me get this right," I reiterate. "You want me to recover some photos from an escort that you were caught with? Does she have a pimp or a boyfriend?

"How do I know you are not setting me up to take the fall so you can protect your godly image? What is the verse in the Bible that says you should cut off your hand if it causes you to sin?" I ask. "You might need to go ahead and resign as a pastor, because your love for pussy is stronger than your love for God. I guess you will have to circumcise yourself to make it to heaven," I state.

"There you go making jokes again, man," Carlos says, "but my money isn't laughing. You will be paid well for your services tonight. Now, she doesn't have a pimp, but the woman that took the picture, her name is Asperilla. She's the ringleader of these ladies. I just need to rattle their business and show them that Pastor Johnson is not the one to be taken lightly. Plus, they had the nerve to show up at my church yesterday morning! I'll call Cherry now and tell her to meet me at the hotel, but you will be the one in the room. All you have to do is keep the room dark, because she'll pick up the key from the front desk. I have been seeing her for over three months now, and the routine is always the same."

I watch as he calls her cell phone, but it goes straight to voicemail. He tells me to be quiet as he leaves a message telling her to meet him at the hotel around midnight. He tells me he'll text me once she's confirmed that she'll be there.

"Man, are you sure this woman will be there?" I ask.

"When it comes to money," he says, "this chick will be there with a trench coat and heels on. She is always greedy, and I have paid her more money than I have given my wife this month so, trust me, she will be at the hotel."

He gives me the hotel address and tells me not to hurt anyone, just shake her up a little. He goes back to his safe and gets me some blood money to do his dirty work. He must be the only pastor in the world that keeps a bill counter in his office. I love him like a brother, but he better pray like hell I'm never in a bind, because he might be the first person I rob.

He finishes running the last bill through the counter and hands me $1,500 for tonight. He smiles and tells me thanks for being there for him when he needs me and that he will call me later this week once everything dies down.

I thanked him and we walk out the office door, leaving behind plenty of dark secrets. I told Carlos that he needs to go home and snuggle up to that beautiful wife of his before someone takes her from under his nose.

He gives me the same retarded line about how God placed them together, and no man would ever take her from him.

I just laugh because that was one of the corniest lines a fool could say, especially if he is out in the streets and leaving her alone at home to satisfy her own needs.

He tells me to stay alert and don't smoke any weed until I'm done with Cherry.

"Don't worry," I tell him, "I got this shit under control."

We drive away from the parking lot in opposite directions.

Looks like tonight I'll be dickin' down somebody's daughter.

The hell with Carlos. I'm lighting up a blunt right now. He should know me better than that. There is nothing wrong with vaporizing my lungs. I am about to get so high that the DJ on the radio will inhale the contact.

I will be on my best behavior tonight, and I hope Strawberry (or was her name Cherry?) is on hers. I wonder if she has some good pussy and a fantastic mouthpiece. I know she has to be fine because Carlos would never fuck with an ugly woman.

The radio starts playing the perfect song by Mystikal, *I Smell Smoke*. I begin to bounce in my seat, puffing and blowing it out the window.

Yeah, I know I will serve this woman my dick. I might even tie her to the bed and make her pussy smoke this blunt in my face. Best believe the pastor ain't the only one with an Indiana Jones' ego. I am going to raid the ark tonight to see what treasure this hoe has between her thighs. Then again, I might just take the pictures and make her walk down the hall naked or something.

Hell, I don't know what I'm going to do, but before I get too high, I need to call my girl and tell her that I'll see her later on this week.

CHAPTER 6
CHERRY

"Cherry, I really don't understand why you're out here hustling dicks on the side," Ayanna says as she gives me a warm hug. "We are not hurting for money at all. If you would have stayed with me that night, the preacher incident wouldn't never have happened. Did you have any idea that Asperilla's crazy ass would bust in the room and start taking pictures and shit? I really don't trust her ass, and the only thing I am asking you is to be careful from now on."

"Ayanna," I reply, "I know you're looking out for me, and I thank you, but I am old enough to make my own decisions. I am selling this city some world-class pussy, so trouble comes with the territory."

"Cherry," she says seriously, "I will level with you about this escort business. I am not trying to stay in this game until dust comes outta my ass. I'm leaving sooner than you think. I enjoyed my time, rode a few dicks, and stacked enough paper to open up my own business. I hope you didn't think I was going to school during the day for nothing. I study hard, and I made these weak men's dicks hard during the night. I'm not proclaiming that I'm perfect, but I refuse to be caught up in other people's bullshit. I'm just saying that you need to get what you can and get the hell out of this business. Even Malakai is making moves to get out the game."

"Easy for him to say when he isn't the one lying on his back or dusting up his knees," I say defiantly.

"I agree with you, but we weren't forced to do this. To be honest, our lifestyle is better than most ladies that work a nine to five. Hell, if we had insurance, we would be the shit!"

We burst out laughing.

"Ayanna, I really appreciate you being the sister that I never had, and, yes, I am hardheaded at times, but I will do my best to stay out of trouble."

Ayanna walks out of the room.

"Yeah, right," I mutter to myself, "staying out of trouble will be harder since that bitch Asperilla is pulling the strings."

I get dressed for tonight, because I have a date with a sexy-ass brother who packs nine inches of steel. It's amazing how a piece of meat can upgrade your whole day. I'll keep an eye out from now on, and I might breakdown and tell Malakai the crazy shit his girl has me doing.

I knew I was in the wrong that night, allowing one of the clients to introduce me to Molly. As Rick James would say, "That's one hell of a drug." The only wild part of that night was how the police found me so quick.

Malakai keeps a tight payroll, so his ladies are usually free to escort anywhere in the city. When I went to jail, Asperilla was the first one on the scene ready to post my bail. I have been her fucking sex slave whenever she needed me to make extra money. I even knew the preacher scandal was coming, but I just played my part. I just pray like hell that I can clear my name with Malakai.

Ayanna might have been smart by saving her money, but I've been spending my shit faster than the nuts I bust. They always say, *where there's a will, there's a way*, so I'll just let tomorrow take care of itself.

"You love this good pussy, don't you? Taste just like cherry pie. Dig all into my shit and make me cum, you bastard. You love when I feed your face," I tell one of my favorite clients. He loves for me to ride his face.

He keeps trying to get me to marry him, but I just ain't the settling down type of woman, so I just continue busting nuts down his nose. I grabbed him by the back of the head and ride his face. I am going to give his ass whiplash as I twirl my hips into his forehead.

This man's tongue is like windshield wipers, running all types of speed as he swipes back and forth, in and out. I love it as he moans and groans all in me. I begin to do my war chant as I cum, because Indian pussy makes this man rain. I poured out my juices all over his face.

He gets off the bed, grabs the Chief headdress from floor and stands up, "Me Geronimo. Me jump in pussy now," he says with his arm across his chest.

I always laugh when he does this wild shit, but I also know in a few minutes he is about to tomahawk my pussy to hell.

He flips me over onto my stomach, and I rest on my knees so he can dive in with lighting thrusts.

He grabs me by my shoulders as he opens me up.

"When I buck forward," he whispers in my ear, "you betta throw that pussy back."

"Yes, Chief Geronimo," I moan.

He starts out with a nice slow grind, and my job as his stubborn horse is to try to throw him off my ass. This is a wild game for those who need a little excitement in their bedroom. This dude believes in serving, and I can feel all his inches easing into me one by one. Every inch feels so fucking good.

I squeeze my muscles around his head to arouse my pleasure. I am ready for the beating he is about to slay me with. He starts to yell as he pounds in and out of my pussy like a hammer into a nail. My mouth begins to drip saliva, and I almost bite my tongue.

He rises up and drags me halfway off the bed, leaving nothing but my ass hanging off. He slowly pushes my face into the mattress and just drills me, slapping my ass. Left cheek, then right.

"Geronimo cums in minute," he shouts.

I am no sorry bitch in the sheets, so I am recoiling this ass against his totem pole.

I scream for more. I can feel his sweat dripping on my back, and that only intensifies the fuck. His war chant becomes louder as his breathing increases.

I believe I can feel his dick in my chest, and it is about to break my heart.

He starts to grunt, and his thrusts become deeper and deeper. I can feel his inches coming outta me, then he sprays my ass cheeks with his warm lava.

We get up, laughing after our fuck fantasy.

We take a shower, and I gave him a little head, so he will always know that Cherry pie is the only sweet thing he needs in his life. I dry him off and help him put on his clothes.

"Same Time, Same Bat Channel," he says as he walks out the door.

I laugh and purr like Eartha Kitt as I claw the air, reaching for his face.

Once he's gone, I slowly close the door and jump on the bed. I turn my cell back on to find a voicemail from the pastor telling me to meet him at the usual spot, and he would pay double. I could use the cash to dig my way out of this hole. I texted back and tell him to give me an hour.

"ROLE PLAYING, WILD SEX, AND NASTY NAMES ARE EQUIVALENT TO GETTING MARRIED AND RECITING VOWS AT A WEDDING."

CHAPTER 7

JERROD

I finally got the text from Carlos; I have one hand on my blunt and the other one in my drawers.

Luckily, I didn't have my other stash or I would have been too high to do anything tonight. I know one thing, this damn woman better hand over those photos, or I might just have to slap her ass around a few times. Carlos said she would be arriving by 11:45, so I have about ten minutes to finish smoking this blunt and scare her ass shitless.

Five minutes after I was done, I cut off all the lights, and just waited by the door. After waiting for about two minutes, I heard someone at the door. This hoe must really want this money because she is on time but the only thing, she will be counting is how many nuts I am going to bust in her face. This room will smell like weed so she will know that I am not the Pastor.

Fuck it! I'll just do it my damn way. The door opens and I snatched the first person to walk in.

"What the fuck, let me go!" she yells.

I threw her on the floor and flip the light switch back on and I must say this bitch is fine as fuck. She looks like one of those Pocahontas chicks with that long hair and pretty skin.

"Where the hell is Carlos and who the fuck are you?" she shouts as she gets off the floor. She gets louder, "Pastor or not, someone is going to pay for my services!"

"Bitch, shut the fuck up!" I reply pulling my gun out from behind my back and point it at her ass.

"Now listen here, Cherry, or whatever your name is."

She finally shuts the fuck up, because now she knows she's not in control anymore.

She takes a seat on the bed and says, "My boss will find you and make sure you pay if anything happens to me."

"Who? Asperilla? Fuck her, too!"

She chuckles, "Nah, bitch. Malakai! You couldn't even imagine the deadliest shit he would do if I am harmed or even touched by the scent of your breath."

My mind races back to Carlos, because he lied to me about this woman having a pimp. I knew he couldn't be trusted. I am going to deal with him another day.

"Well, you can sit your bitch ass right there until you give me those pictures," I tell her.

She begins to hum the jeopardy tune in my face. That shit burns me the hell up, and I just can't take it. I did want to fuck but I am over it; I just want to punch her in the fucking throat for talking to me like she lost her damn mind.

"I am going to ask you one more time. Where are the fucking pictures?"

"I don't have them. Asperilla gave them to the pastor yesterday, so you need to let me go," she snaps back.

"What the hell you mean they gave them to the pastor?" I yell.

She tells me that Malakai and Asperilla gave Pastor Johnson the photos back after he paid them the money. This is usually the time I would go light up a blunt, but I have other plans for tonight.

"Cherry, you are an honest hoe. I knew you never had the pictures and I also know that Asperilla and Malakai were fucking during his church services as well. I knew Carlos was full of shit because my source told me everything, but I am going to make an example out of you," I tell her.

If this Malakai dude is so grimy, let's see what he would do if I bruised up one of his ladies and blame the pastor for it.

"You are going to suck this dick," I said as I walk up to her.

"I ain't sucking shit and I am not afraid to die," she replies as she rolls her eyes.

I knew she would say something crazy, so I backhand her with the gun so hard until she stumbles back and fell.

"Bitch, playtime is over for you," I shout.

I put my gun down and began to pull her by the hair. "You and your boss can go to hell, but I am going to send a message to him first. Don't worry, you little hoe, you will live to tell the story," I say to her and then punch her in the stomach.

"You ain't talking shit now, huh, hoe?" I holler. She balls up in a cradle position to protect herself from the blows.

I whisper into her ear, "This ass whipping is being furnished by Pastor Johnson."

I pick her up from the floor and slam her on the bed. I begin to rip off her clothes. I am going to teach them all a lesson for thinking Jerrod is weak.

I snatch her thongs off and stuff it in her mouth. She reaches up and claws my face.

I could feel her nails sinking into my skin. "Aww shit, you stupid trick!" I scream.

"Fuck you," she says as she knees me in the nuts.

I fall onto the floor and her crazy ass jumps on top of me and started to punch me in my face.

I finally had enough of this shit and punched her so hard in the nose that blood and snot flew out. She fell back to the floor stunned from the blow.

I stood up and spit in her face. "Swallow that since you didn't want to swallow this dick."

I left her lying on the floor; grab my things and the money so I could make it rain on her pathetic ass before I walk out the door.

I took one last look back and knew the damage I cause would come back to Carlos, but at this moment, I didn't give a fuck and I walk out the door.

CHERRY

"Fuck, I am in all types of pain," I groan as I lift myself off the floor. I reached for my purse and pulled out my cell phone. I dial Ayanna number and she answers.

"I need your help," I moaned to her.

"Cherry, where the hell are you?" Ayanna shouted.

I finally mustered up enough strength to tell her that I am at the Sailport Suite in Rocky Point, and I was set up by Pastor Johnson.

"What room are you in?" Ayanna asks hysterically.

"I am in Room 626. Please hurry."

"I will be there in about twenty minutes," Ayanna says as she rushes off the phone.

I couldn't imagine that after being dick down by one of my clients that I would be setup by another man. "Damn you, Asperilla!" I scream. "This is your fault that I was attack."

I slowly walked to the bathroom so I could take a look at my face. I was horrified by the sight of the bruises that bastard left. I have a black eye, as well, but at least I have all of my teeth.

Oh yeah, this guy will face the death penalty real soon, and I am going to get his ass. I refuse to be a woman that allows a man to use me as a punching bag and get away with it; "Hell nah!"

I run the water from the sink, wash my face, then I sit on the toilet seat until I hear a knock at the door. The knocking becomes louder without pause. I grab the side of my ribs and force myself to walk through the room. I knew it was Ayanna because of the screaming and yelling.

"Open the door, Cherry!" Ayanna shouted.

I open the door and Ayanna storms inside. She walks over to me and notices the bruises on my face.

"This man will pay for this shit!" Ayanna screams.

I told her don't worry, and that I managed to sneak in a punch or two; plus, Malakai will find him.

"Ayanna, help me put on my damn clothes so you can take me to the emergency room," I moan.

We get on the elevator and press the button to the main floor. It seems like it took forever to reach the front lobby.

The truck was parked in front of the building, and she helped me into the passenger seat. Ayanna closes the door and I tap the button to let down the window. Ayanna walks to the other side, gets in the truck, and starts it up.

"Cherry, I will have you at the emergency room in a little while. Just relax," Ayanna states as she picks up the phone to call Malakai.

"Damn that shit went to voicemail. Asperilla probably cut his phone off," she said angrily. "I'll just call him in the morning."

She started up the truck and the wind from the night air felt good as she drove off.

I begin with my earlier thought. "I'll let tomorrow take care of itself, but who the hell will take care of me today?"

CHAPTER 8

MALAKAI

I woke up with a pussy hangover. I get those from sticking my tongue so deep inside of a woman that the juice can have the same effects as hard liquor. Now my head is hurting, but I did fuck Asperilla into a coma last night. I'm going to relax all day, spend some time with my woman, and maybe treat her to a lovely evening.

But before I can even enjoy the idea, my phone rings.

"Yeah, this is Malakai--" Before I can finish my words, Ayanna starts screaming in the phone.

"That damn dude jumped on Cherry last night, and we had to take her to the emergency room!"

"What damn dude?"

"Some dude that knew Pastor Johnson. He hemmed Cherry up at the hotel over those photos."

"Ayanna," I say, "just relax and calm down. How is Cherry doing?"

"Well, he broke her nose and gave her a black eye, but she'll survive."

"Thanks for the call. I thought that damn pastor would have stopped messing with that side pussy after the last time. Niggas never learn until it's their time to burn. I'll be over there today, Ayanna," I say and hang up the phone.

Damn, I think to myself, *this was supposed to be a day off without drama.*

I look over at Asperilla as she wakes up. "What's wrong, babe?" she asks.

"Fuck, you are!" I shouted "You and these stupid ass schemes for more money have caused the pastor to retaliate and Cherry was attacked last night. I need to go handle his ass for real this time. That damn dude doesn't know when to quit."

"I'm sorry for getting the girls mixed up in this," she says.

"Whatever, Asperilla. I told you not to put these girls in harm's way. You have enough money; sit your crazy ass down somewhere."

I know, deep in my mind, that a situation like this can never happen again.

"Don't worry, I got this. You are going to find your ass in this life without me."

I rolled out of bed and hit the shower. I'm so pissed.

I did a lot of thinking while the water was running. I have to get even with the pastor before I kill his ass and I know the perfect way to do it.

I finish showering, get out and get dressed.

I look over at Asperilla and tell her that we will finish this conversation later when I return.

I grabbed my keys and headed out the door. I figure today is a beautiful day to see the First Lady.

I might be coldblooded, but no worries. I am only going to kill her with this dick. Since the whole city's always talking about that ass, I'm going to sample a small taste.

I will drive my Escalade this morning because I love being in the smoky black ride. I've already done my homework on the First Lady. Before the escort service, I actually attended their church.

She was always sexy, and today I'm planning to get everything the pastor owes me, paid back in full by his wife.

I drive down the interstate and take the exit that will lead me to the church. I pull up and just wait in the church parking lot.

My timing couldn't have been any better and I knew she would have a morning class, so I'll wait until it's over before I make my move.

I looked at my watch and it read 10:45 AM. All the other ladies were leaving the church and within ten minutes, the First Lady came outside carrying some bags.

I run over, "Excuse me, do you need some help?" I ask.

"No, thank you. I'm fine."

"You didn't let me finish," I say with a grin. "Do you need some help getting out of those clothes?"

"Young man," she says with a smile, "evidently your parents never taught you how to speak to a woman."

"Yes, you're right. Excuse me, ma'am, do you need some help getting out of those clothes?"

She looks at me strangely, "You're that poet, Malakai. I've seen your pictures on a few of my young ladies Facebook pages.

Your mother should have taught you to leave your shirt on sometimes."

"The one and only at your service, and today is the day I make you a woman."

"Boy, please. I was a woman before your mama let you out of her womb."

I just keep smiling and for a woman that's forty-four, she's got everything going for herself. Deep down I know she's still a freak.

"You don't want any of your members to drive up and see you out here talking to me," I say, "and if you really want to get rid of that problem, then follow me."

"What problem are you talking about? And Jesus will fix every problem that I have." she says.

I laugh, "You're right, but I know something you need fixing, and I am the perfect maintenance man for the job. I know Carlos isn't taking care of your sexual wants and desires."

"How do you know what's happening inside of my home and why are you here anyway?" she proclaims.

"I am here to give you an opportunity of a lifetime with no strings attached. If I can't get you wet with a few words, then I will leave and never return."

She smiles again. I know she's hooked, and I am about to stimulate her ears.

"Okay, Mrs. Tasha. Are you ready?" I asked.

"Go ahead, Mr. Malakai, because I am in love with only God's words."

"Well, you are in for a treat because where do you think I get all these beautiful words from?" I asked her.

I cleared my throat and began to speak.

Adam dived in face first,
Came up dripping with hunger and thirst.
Her fruit, her nectar is all over him,
And she screams for more.
Eve, all of a sudden, turns into a wild animal, Scratching,
clawing, and biting Adam with all of her might. Adam resists the
pain
Because he is searching for her inner flame.
He is determined to make sure the first orgasm
Is deeper than the flood in the next chapter.
If God is going to give Moses a staff,
Then he must have blessed his tongue
To be the aftermath.
That means he will leave her like a desert drought
When he blows her back out.
Adam continues to blow the fire out.
He is so deep; he can walk through her mind
And speak to her thoughts.
Eve screams and lets out a final moan
The earth started to shake, trees started to break,
The animals start howling, barking, and running.
Adam kept gunning because he refused to let go

Of his grip until he caught the last sip.
He rose up with her juices dripping down to the ground. Eve
lay motionless but blessed.
God called Adam and said well done.
That's what I created love for.

When I was finished, I could tell by the look in her eyes that it has been a long time since Carlos, or any man caused her body to shift in another direction.

I grab the bags from her hand and say if you want to know how that poem begins, then follow me. I knew she wanted to fuck, church woman or not, no woman wants to be cheated on. Sometimes, all it takes is to be the right man, or shall I say poet with words, in the right place.

She was so speechless that she went straight to her car and turned around with the *ok* gesture.

I smile because she forgot her bags; I guess she will get them from me once we reach the destination.

I went to my car, started it up and drove off to my destination with my cougar right behind me.

We pull up to one of many fuck houses. I exit my truck and walk over to her car and open her door. I led her up the walkway, unlocked the door and escorted her inside. I politely asked her to have a seat. I'm going to videotape the First Lady. Unlike rookies, my fuck houses have cameras all around the place; I never know when I might need to get away and watch movies from the past.

I decided to fix myself a drink, and she tells me she has to be home real soon because of another engagement; it wouldn't be good for a First Lady to be late.

She has on this sundress that comes right below her knees with these cute 4-inch Vince Camuto wedges.

The pastor is a dumbass, but I thank him. I finished my drink and ask her for a kiss. She leans in.

"First Lady, I want them other lips."

She smiles. "Take them, they are yours for now."

I pick her up and carry her to the bedroom. I slowly undress her 'til she's naked, and I take off my clothes. I picked her up, and let her legs straddle my waist.

I begin to suck her left earlobe while I cupped her breast with my hands.

She moans sweet sounds of joy, so I know it feels good.

I flick my tongue around her nipples, then pause and start to suck on them slowly and smooth.

She's begging me to take her, all of her.

I keep fore playing her soul, switching between nipples.

"I love this," she cries. "It's been so long since a man has taken me into ecstasy."

I glide my tongue down her waist, hips, and thighs until I reach her clit. I dive in headfirst, sucking the almonds out of her joy. The First Lady's soul has a sweet taste, and my tongue is clinging to her juices.

I knew the freak inside of her would come out.

"Fuck me right now," she says. "I need to feel your dick inside of me."

It's actually a turn on to hear a First Lady say those words. She let out a scream as she cums on my tongue. I come up for air, throw her legs over my shoulders, and slowly insert my dick into her wet pussy. I slowly rock her with nice, deep strokes.

"Fuck this pussy, Mr. Poet!" she shouts.

So, I started to shift gears and began to thrust harder and faster.

I pushed her legs so far back that she could suck on her own damn toes. I'm all in that pussy, slanging this dick harder and harder.

"I want to ride this dick," she says.

We flip over, and the First Lady gets on top, and I mean she rides the saddle off this dick. She grabs the back of my head and goes into a squat position and bounces up and down on my dick. I push her in and out of me. She is working that pussy so hard until the sweat from her forehead is dripping on my chest.

I give her a reason to say, "Oh my God," and she ain't even in church right now.

She screams, "Make me cum!"

I arch my back up every time she crashes down on my dick.

She moans one last time and cums all over my sheets. I kept stroking until I shot my load right back at her.

She just lays on my chest for a minute and whispered in my ear, "I am so glad that you came to the church today. I really needed to feel sexy again."

I must admit, First Lady has some good pussy. Best believe this will not be the last time she hears of Malakai.

She finally gets off my chest, goes and takes a shower and comes out looking like new money.

She gets dressed and tells me thanks for a wonderful time.

"Do you need me to see you home safe?" I ask like a gentleman.

"I'll be okay," she says with a smile.

I watch her car leave the driveway, close the door, and went back to rewind the camera of our sex session.

"Another one bites the dust."

I know I have to check on my girls, so I call Ayanna and tell her that I'll be over there in about an hour.

I take a quick shower, get dressed, and run out the door. I jump in the truck and head over to their apartment. I make it over there in about 30 minutes.

I pulled up to the house and knock on the door. My girls don't live on the street corners, and I'll be damned if I let them stay in some torn down crack house. It's very important that you protect your investments. They are the reason why I ball like I do. I have ladies in every city where I own a spoken word spot. I have my bottom bitches run the game when I'm out of town, and they get paid well. They could probably leave me and start their own business, but they love working for me. We're like a family.

Ayanna opens the door and I walk in; I see Cherry a little bruised up but she's happy to see me.

These girls have everything going for them. Cherry is one of the sexiest Native Americans I've ever laid eyes on. She's from Wyoming, so I have no idea how the hell she ended up in Florida, but I had to have her on my team from the moment I saw her.

Ayanna is from Atlanta, and she's a dime peach with everything you could want in a woman.

All my ladies stay two to a household. I never keep the same breed of woman together because I want them to learn from and trust each other. That's my secret: never board ladies of the same background together. Hell, even I have a Russian and a Caribbean woman living together in New York.

I tell them, "The Pastor will pay for this and I will make sure to catch the guy that attacked you. Just leave everything to me and I promise that you will have your revenge. I also promise that this will never happen again."

I apologize to Cherry for Asperilla putting her in this situation.

I say sympathetically, "I'll be in touch and everything will be alright."

They smile and give me a hug.

"We love you, Malakai," they say together.

I walk out the door, get into my car, pick up my cell and call Kryptonite. He answers after the third ring.

"Well, if it isn't the wild ass poet/pimp," he chuckles.

"Yeah, whatever. I need you to catch a plane next week to Tampa and help ease my mind."

"What the fuck's wrong with your ass now?" he questions.

"I'll explain everything when you get here."

"No problem, see you soon," he said.

We hung up the phone; I put in some Jill Scott's *A Long Way Home* and hit the highway.

"EVERY WOMAN LOVES A MAN WITH A GOOD CONVERSATION, BUT SHE LOVES HIM MORE WHEN HE EATS HER OUT AND LISTENS TO HER MOAN."

CHAPTER 9

MALAKAI

It has been a whole week since Asperilla and I have spoken. We will talk later on today after I leave the airport and squash the pastor drama she caused.

Kryptonite's flight comes in around noon and I am anxious to see the man who I consider a father since I never had one. We have a lot to get caught up on, especially old times.

The airport is busy, like always, but I can see him flashing that million-dollar smile from a mile away.

"Malakai," he says instead of a greeting, "what's the urgency of me coming out here?"

"Asperilla's schemes backfired and one of my ladies was attacked because of the bullshit," I explain. "No worries. I only flew you out here for company, not to kill this time."

"Malakai, that woman is going to be the death of you one day. She is a money hungry demon; you better start watching your back because I don't trust her."

"Asperilla is Asperilla and we have been together a long time. She does stupid shit but her ass is loyal. She is my ride or die chick and I love her crazy ass," I proudly say.

"Yeah. Whatever, fool. Help me with these bags," Kryptonite says while shaking his head.

I help him with his bags and we head straight to my truck.

"I spared the Pastor's life once but this time, I am about to crucify his ass," I said boldly.

"Do you still have those Chinese twins' phone numbers? The ones that we ran up on in Miami?" he asks. "They were packing more heat than us. Call them up and let them deal with the Pastor, and we will end this charade once and for all."

We cruise from the airport and head down to this nice Italian restaurant and enjoy the day. We catch up on old times, and it's like a family reunion with this guy all over again.

I made the call to the twins.

"Wassup, Mei?" I ask as soon as the phone picks up.

"At your fucking service, Malakai. You need us for one of your parties, huh?" she chuckles.

"Yes, I need y'all to come to Tampa ASAP," I say.

"We're in Miami again," she tells me, "but we can catch a flight tonight."

"Cool. You can call me when y'all arrive and get settled," I say as I hang up the phone.

These twins will do just fine to substitute for the Pastor's masseuse. His eyes and dick will expand to the damn wall when he sees these two fine-ass twins.

"Malakai," Kryptonite says, "sometimes the price of taking one's soul can take a toll on a man. You're still young, and you have enough money to last for a long time. You need to think about getting out the business and do what makes you happy."

I know he's talking about my spoken word.

We finished our lunch and head towards my house.

"Hell nah," Kryptonite says, "I refuse to stay with Asperilla. I got deep love for you, but you know we don't get along."

"No problem, man. You can stay at one of my condos downtown. Everything you'll need is already here. Enjoy Tampa."

"Man, that's what I'm talking about. We have to catch up tomorrow; I am tired from that flight," he says, yawning.

I get out and help him with his bags. "I owe you again," I tell him.

"Yeah, your debt is overflowing," he says.

We hugged and laughed; I jump in the Hummer and head home.

---------------------******---------------------

ASPERILLA

I love that nigga, but, truthfully, I will forever love the money. I have a nice percentage from all the deals, but a girl always needs more. I just want it all.

Malakai runs this business like it's a fucking union. I despise his ways sometimes. When the ladies work for me, I'll have their asses in a one room apartment, fucking around the clock.

He shares too much with those hoes.

For tonight, though, I pick up the phone and dial the only person that could go toe to toe with Malakai for eating this pussy.

Pandora picks up the phone, and her voice has my snatch soaking wet with each syllable.

I love this chick; she's been on my team for a minute. "What are your plans for tonight?" I ask.

"Nothing, but for you, anything you like," Pandora says.

"Okay I'll meet you at the usual club around ten, and then we can have our own after party." I told her.

"I'll be there with one of my *fuck me* dresses on," she says and hangs up the phone.

Pandora is one of those sexy ass freaks, 5'6", 140, and thick all over. I met her five years ago when she used to strip in Miami, and our chemistry was on fire from the first moment we laid eyes on each other. We've being fucking on the side ever since that magical night. I know Malakai probably knows the truth, but he's so business minded, he just doesn't give a damn. I'll just tell him that I'm spending the night over at her house. He's with Kryptonite anyway, so I'm sure he won't mind me being out tonight.

I'll find something sexy to wear tonight to stop them in mid-step before I get some head.

Yes, Asperilla, you are still one fine-ass muthafucker, and that will never change!

I'll apologize to Malakai later, but he needs to understand that before the ladies came in the picture, I was always the Queen around this muthafucker.

I've worked my ass off to get to where I am today. I grew up poor as hell in Tijuana. My mama used to turn tricks, and then came to the states to clean hotels for a living. I'll be damned if I sweep or mop anything in this world. She always told me I'd never go broke as long as I used what I had between my thighs, and my beautiful face. I know I am twice as sexy as the vixen, Kristal Solis. Mama told me to remember that my pussy is a masterpiece.

I turn on the radio, and Maxwell is playing. He is so sexy. I do a little dance while I groove to his music and prepare to meet Pandora. We'll drink, fuck, drink, and just get high as hell and cum the night away. Tonight is all about Asperilla.

-----------------------෨෨෨෨෨෨-----------------------

MALAKAI

As soon as I open the front door, Asperilla runs out of it.

This silly woman almost knocks me down. "Damn, is it that serious?"

"Pandora and I are having a ladies night out tonight." She pats her hands between her legs. "No men allowed."

She always runs to Pandora whenever we have a disagreement. I tell her to be careful and we will talk later. I've always wondered if those two freaks are bumping coochies together. I wouldn't put it pass them.

I need my rest anyway, because the twins are due in later and I have to brief them on the plan. Nothing is free so I have to have the money on hand as well.

I grab my laptop and sink my mind into other poets' work. I love reading the inspiration of others.

After reading poetry for two hours, my phone rings.

"Hello," I say.

"We are here, meet us at Ballast Point Park," they anxiously say before hanging up the phone.

They want to meet at a damn park of all places, late at night. They're thirsty for killing, and they are ready to add another head to their trophy case. Meiying and Mei are some of China's best secrets. *More like secret assassins*, I thought to myself. There's no turning back now.

I grabbed my keys and headed out the door. The traffic was light tonight and I made it there in 15 minutes.

I pulled up to the park. It is dark as hell, but I can hear them talking in the shadows. I approach them with the money, handing it over. We discuss the way I want things to go.

"Is it all there?" Mei asks. "Because it is too dark to be counting money."

"Yeah," I say, "everything you need is there."

"Just like men," Meiying says, "always need a woman to clean up their dirty messes. Dude, are you getting soft? I remember when you wouldn't even spend a dollar for a hit."

"I know ya'll are trying to get inside of my head," I laugh.

Crazy bitches. I love money, but I'm not damn possessed by it. I plan on leaving the business as quickly as possible.

"Back to business, ladies," I say, pulling their attention. "I would do this myself but I love adding thrill to a kill. I need you all to dress up as masseuses, seduce and kill someone for me."

"Fuck yeah! Sounds like our type of work," Mei shouts.

"I knew you would enjoy this one. I will recon the place, give you all the details on him, and all you have to do is finish him off."

"No problem; anything for you, with your fine chocolate ass," they say.

"There's extra money for you all to enjoy Tampa; I will send a text or call once I have everything in place. The timeline is one week. If you need me, don't hesitate to hit me up," I insist.

"Shit! We were hoping that you would have said tomorrow. Now I have to stop the pulse in my pussy from jumping around," said Meiying while pouting.

And they say that I am sick… I guess I hang with some psychotic people.

We finish the transaction and walk away in opposite directions. I'll have one less headache soon.

"KILLER PUSSY DOESN'T ALWAYS REFER TO SEX. SOMETIMES IT'S TWO WOMEN THAT WILL KILL FOR MONEY WHILE YOUR DICK IS HARD AS A ROCK."

CHAPTER 10

PASTOR JOHNSON

I am feeling good today since my lawyer is visiting this morning. It will be quiet to discuss business because Tasha is at the church promoting the ideas for the Annual Women's Conference. It has been a week and Jerrod hasn't called; I wonder if he found out that I lied about the pictures and Malakai.

If I had told him the truth, he probably wouldn't have taken care of that problem, but I wanted revenge more than friendship. I pray this fool didn't do anything stupid. I know he is probably high, but he always comes through for me; I'll just wait. If something did go wrong, Asperilla, that damn devil, would have been blowing up my spot by now, so I'll just let everything blow over.

The doorbell rings and I am eager to put this plan into action so I can clear up the situation that happened at the church. Mr. Wakefield walked in with his briefcase and didn't crack a smile or even speak.

I think to myself, *I am paying you to help me; you could at least say hello when you walk into my home.*

He sits down and pulls out the paperwork. "Good Morning, Pastor Johnson."

"Morning," I reply. "Would you like some coffee or tea?"

"Not today. I want to discuss this issue, because I want this story to air on the evening news."

I tell him, "I am listening to every word, prepared to do or pay whatever to make this official."

"Samantha Brooks wants to headline your story which could help catapult her from street reporter to top anchor at the station. I need for you to grab a few young adults, that will do anything for cash, to enhance your story so we will deflect the attention off your church," he insists.

"She will interview the ushers at the movies, who will also want a piece of the pie, so you have to include them in as well.

"Now this is the best part of the plan, I will bring two outsiders to your church as the sex cult leaders. They will repent about fucking in your office and thank you for saving their life.

"We will set up a small camera team to record it and you will look like the perfect saint. Problem solved; any questions?" he concluded.

"No questions at all," I say as I stand up, escorting him to the door with a twisted smile.

"Pastor Johnson, you really need to fly right. But every time you tilt, the balance in my checking account goes up," he laughs.

"Mr. Wakefield, enjoy this last payout because I am turning over a new leaf after this one," I say.

I shook his hand and told him that he will be compensated for his services.

I watch as he walks out the house, gets into his car, and drives through the gate. I am done with this side life. I decide to pick up some things from the store to prepare a beautiful lunch for my wife.

It's time I started treating her like the Queen that she is.

----------------------෨෨෨෨෨෨-----------------------

TASHA

"Excuse me, First Lady," she interrupts. "I hate to interrupt this meeting, but the Sisters and I are concerned about the incident during service two Sundays ago. I covered up my daughter's ears so she couldn't hear that Jezebel moaning and groaning. Pastor needs to get a hold of his church or we will vote him out!"

I have to rein in my temper before I end up smacking the crap out of this woman.

"I know what happened," I stand up and say, "We are all grown and living in a polluted world. Let me sprinkle a little knowledge on all of you. The world was corrupt in the Bible, men wanted to have sex with the angels God sent to destroy the city. Even when Lot offered his daughters to the men, they still wanted the angels. This crazy sex cult just happened to hit our church."

Thinking to myself, *I can't believe I'm taking up for my triflin' ass husband.*

"Now, I do ask that God remove the sounds of sex from your child's ears, but for you to speak about voting out the pastor is just ridiculous. You and I both know that you aren't clean. But don't worry, I won't tell your business. And in return, you will keep my husband's name out of your mouth," I dictate.

She shrinks in her seat as I jump down her throat.

"This meeting is adjourned. If anyone has anything else to say, feel free to speak," I demand.

They all calmly decline but offer to pray for the church and the members.

I smile, "Thank you. Now I ask that we all join hands and pray."

We finish praying, exchange hugs, and leave the church.

I went to my car and start crying. I never asked to be a First Lady. Yes, I love church, and singing is my passion, but I just wanted to be a normal Christian out of the spotlight. All of that changed when I met Carlos at a revival. He was so handsome, and his preaching was phenomenal and gifted. I was drawn in by his words. He invited me to his church a few times, and after a few Sundays, he asked me out on a date. That's my life in a nutshell. Since then, that man has caused more than a few problems.

I pull down the visor and stare into the mirror to see my mascara running. I know my husband is out of control, but who was I to judge? I had sex with that poet, and, God, if you are listening, it felt so good, too. I'm tired of living this perfect life, being the 'Perfect First Lady,' while my husband runs the streets. I gave my life to You, and You gave me Solomon's evil twin, because he collects ladies like coins. God, I need a sign or something, because I will serve You faithfully, but You need to show me something.

Out of nowhere, the radio came on playing Shekinah Glory's *YES*. I begin to cry and sing as the words begin to pour out of my soul.

Open up your heart and Tell the Lord: Yes!
Say: Yes, yeah yeah!
Say: I'll obey, Jesus, I won't stray, Jesus,
But this time I've made up in my mind,
I've made up in my mind.
I'll say, say, say, Yes! My soul says yes,
My mind says,
My heart says yes, yes, Yes,
I will, Jesus, Yes, Yes!
I'll do what You want me to do,
I'll say what You want me to say,
I'll go, if You lead me,
If you lead me, if you lead me, if you lead me,
If you lead me, I'll go, yes!

I start speaking in a daze. "Lord, I know there is more that You require of me, and what better song could You have used as a sign for me to do Your will?"

I wipe the last of my tears, but now tears of pure joy and strength. I pray again and ask for forgiveness before I start my car.

I know that He is truly God, and He deserves all of my praise. Thank you, Jesus!

I keep singing as I start the car and drive down the street. For the first time in a long time, I feel complete and real about my ministry.

PASTOR JOHNSON

The store is beyond crowded today, but I made it. Now, I am about to celebrate my victory lunch with the most beautiful woman in the world. If I weren't a pastor, I probably could be a chef. My chicken marsala tastes like a piece of heaven with a nice bottle of white wine to lighten up the day.

I believe every woman deserves something to make her blush and feel appreciated; I even have balloons all over the den with the words *I love you, Tasha* written on them. The woman that works in the gift department has made a lot of money from me over the years. The table is set, and I have a little music playing.

The atmosphere is perfect for this lunch date, and I can imagine the smile on her face when she steps into the room.

I hear the car coming through the gates, and I run to the window like a peeping little kid. I grab my final surprise and stand in the middle of the floor to wait.

She walks and sees the balloons and lunch, her whole expression changes. To top it off, I pull out a teddy bear hiding behind my back.

"You are so amazing!" she says as she kisses me.

I embraced her like it was our first-time meeting all over again, and I don't want to let her go.

"You are so sweet, Carlos," she says with another kiss.

"Follow me, baby," I say as I escort her to her seat. I walk into the kitchen, fix her plate, and bring a red rose with her favorite wine.

"Where is your plate, Carlos?" she asks with concern.

I smile, "I am going to make sure my wife receives the pampering that she deserves."

I serve her and take the fork to stir the marsala. I slowly glide the first bite to her mouth, and with one taste, she moans in delight. "Carlos, this is really delicious! You outdid yourself this afternoon," she says with a mouthful.

"And this is only the first of many days to come. I owe you so much. Please, allow me to become a servant to you for the rest of our marriage," I say as I kiss her hand.

Tasha looks me right in the eyes, "You are amazing at times, but I am not stupid. You have a lot to fix around the church and this home."

I respond with a kiss on her cheek. "Just call me and I'll wait on you on hand and foot."

I finish feeding her, and we start sipping a little wine and talk. "How was your day at the church this morning?" I ask.

"Messy as usual, but nothing that a First Lady can't handle. Talking about the location and price of the Annual Women's

Conference; we're in the process of finalizing the plans to do this in another month."

"I love the idea, and I know it will be a success and a blessing to so many women," I say proudly.

We talk as I clean the table and wash the remaining dishes.

I lead her into the entertainment room saying, "Baby, just relax, lie down and I will slip off your heels."

I massage her feet until she falls asleep. After about ten minutes, I slowly drift off.

I wake up and check my watch. It's 6:15 pm. I almost cuss, but I control myself.

"Carlos, what is wrong? Why are you jumping around like a crack head on steroids?"

"Baby, I just remembered the news is coming on today about the sex cult. I think this news will help ease their minds about my involvement."

I flip the channel and catch the special right on time.

"Good evening. I am Samantha Brooks with Bay News 9, and I am here at the CinéBistro with one of the ushers, Tim Wright, who witnessed a scene with the sex cult that has swept into our city. Tim, would you kindly tell us what was seen?"

"I was going to clean up the movie theater, like I always do, and as soon as I got in there, I heard moaning and groaning. I just thought the movie was still on, but, my God, I saw legs in the air. As I shined my flashlight, they started getting dressed and took off running. One of the guys sucker-punched me as they charged out of the theater. I want everyone out there to take a look at my damn swollen eye.

"There had to be like four or five groups in there. I tried to run after them, but they hit the streets so quick. I didn't get a good look at them. I just pray that this thing stops real soon. This is bad for business."

"Thank you, Mr. Wright," she says. "This sex cult is not only performing acts in theaters and stores, but they have also hit up one of Tampa's largest congregations. Yes, you heard it here— members of the cult were heard having sex at Mt. Liberty Baptist Church earlier this month. We believe that the male and female that were at the church are the ringleaders, and they are having people perform these acts as initiation into the group. I am Samantha Brooks, reporting live at CinéBistro. Back to you."

"I told you, Tasha, I had nothing to do with that couple having sex in the church. Now I just pray for peace among the members," I say as I bow my head.

Tasha leans over and kisses me. One day, I will get tired of plotting and lying, but that day will be next week. I just have to wait for my lawyer to fly in the couple to pull off the church scene.

I smile back and give my wife a wet kiss as we go upstairs for the rest of the evening.

"A MAN WHO CHEATS CAN FLIP MORE LIES THAN A SKILLED ACROBAT"

CHAPTER 11
PASTOR JOHNSON

Today is the big meeting at the church. I called everyone in town to this one. I even have my lawyer there for support, and, once again, Jerrod is not answering his damn phone. I guess I'll call him when I need the fool again. The house is packed, and I know some people are only here to be nosy. That's cool with me, because they are about to get a sermon and a little singing today.

I refuse to make the ring leaders of the group look bad. I plan on lifting them up, so everyone can see that the pastor is a forgiving man, even when his reputation is on the line. I wait until everyone takes their seats.

"Good evening, Saints," I say politely.

The members shout back, "Evening, Pastor!"

"I truly thank you all for coming out this evening, and I understand that some of you have been troubled for the past few weeks. Tonight, we will address all of your concerns and settle your curiosity about the incident. I know some members stand with me and some against me, but I stand in faith and rooted in His word that victory shall be won tonight.

"God has placed on my heart to not lay blame tonight, but to heal people's hearts and minds. If the world wants to see change, then it must start in this church."

"Amen, Pastor," the church cries.

"So tonight, let's give love back to the church like love was given to a dying world. Please worship with me as the choir sings *Take Me to the King*."

The church stands to their feet as the song is ministered to their heart. I begin to sing and the spirit lifts everyone's soul.

> *Truth is it's time*
> *To stop playing these games*
> *We need a word*
> *For the people's pain*
> *So, Lord speak right now*
> *Let it fall like rain*
> *Oh, yeah, we're desperate*
> *We're chasing after you*

I am on fire and ready to preach as I jump up and down as the choir finishes the song.

"Lives will be turned around tonight!" I shouted.

"Yes, Pastor!"

"Since you are already on your feet, please remain standing for the power of God's Word."

I pray, then read Hosea 1:2. "Thus said the Lord when Jehovah spake at the first by Hosea. Jehovah said unto Hosea: 'Go, take unto thee a wife of whoredom and children of whoredom; for the land doth commit great whoredom, departing from Jehovah.'

"I like to use this as a subject. *There are some whores in this house.*"

I can hear the gasps upon the haters' breath when I spoke that title.

"God, the true living God, asked a righteous man to marry a whore. She could be called a promiscuous woman, but I'm keeping it raw and uncut. When rumors are being spread around town, I know some members add extra details. Now, imagine yourself married to this woman who is sleeping with everyone in town; she runs off and leaves you at home with the kids that's probably not even yours. Tell me, what do you do? God wants you to go there and get that woman, that whore, your wife." I preach.

The whole church is stunned. They're glued to the Word, and I am all into it myself, because I know I have been a whore all my life.

"Well, what do you do? God said take fifteen shekels, or fifteen silver coins, some grain and go buy her back from another man. You do as the Word says, even if you don't like it. You do it. So, Hosea marched out to the street and bought the promiscuous woman, the whore, his wife, back. The most important thing about this story is that not only did he buy her back, but he also showed her love for the rest of her days on Earth. So, if we, who are God's people, people that He owns, would rather whore with the things of this world, then why must God Himself come back to buy a wife that He already own after He witnesses us sleeping and lusting after other gods. He came back with a price to bring us out of damnation and back to His loving arms of protection."

I end my sermon and the choir sings.

> *Now that's love. They hung Him high,*
> *They stretched Him wide.*
> *He hung His head, And then He died.*
> *That's love, that's love.*

The choir is finishing up the song as I walk toward the restroom.

I text the couple and ask if they're ready. They respond that they're waiting on my cue. The biggest smile comes to my face as I walk back to the pulpit. The church is still praising and worshipping, so I wait for a few minutes.

After they settle back down, I say, "Once again, I truly appreciate you all for coming. I would like to introduce you to a special couple, Roderick and Malaysia. Please welcome them."

They slowly walk to the altar and I meet them. I greet them with hugs and love. Roderick takes the microphone first, but before he says his first word, I step in.

"Members of Mt. Liberty, please show respect and pride. That means no commotions or discussions during the things they are about to say," I insist.

"Good evening, Saints of Mt. Liberty. My name is Roderick and this is my girlfriend, Malaysia. I beg of you to please listen before you make any assumptions or attack us with verbal hatred. I would like to ask for your forgiveness for the sex act we performed in your church a couple of Sundays ago. It started out as a fun thing to do, but it has gotten out of hand."

One member stands up and yells, "It is beyond out of hand because we have kids that are afraid to come back to church!"

I step back in with the sound of a thousand earthquakes. "You will show respect for these two, or you will be escorted out." I turn back to Roderick. "My brother, please finish your statement."

"Thank you, Pastor. As I was saying, we started this out of boredom, and it became a wild movement. Most of our friends are behind bars now, and the only reason we are here today is because Pastor Johnson decided not to turn us in to the police.

"We agreed to publicly apologize to every member of the church, your family, and your ministry. All I ask is that you please forgive us like He has forgiven us."

This man has put on a performance with tears pouring down his face. Malaysia takes the microphone and makes up a story about never having a father figure. She turned to sex for attention like many other ladies; she needs to pray for abstinence and will only share her soul with her future husband.

"I just ask you all to forgive me like God has, and I promise to never do anything to disrespect your church again," she pleads.

The church stands and claps for the couple.

"Ain't God good?" I shouted.

"Yes, He is, Pastor," he replies.

The deacons escort the actors to my office to save them the trouble of the members getting in their faces.

"If you feel in your heart that I am not worthy to be your spiritual leader. Then I will step down as your Pastor. So, if some of you want to vote me out, please raise your hand."

Not one single hand rises.

CHAPTER 12

MEIYING AND MEI

"Oh, yes, baby, massage this big, black cock. You make me feel so good. Yes, baby, yes. I can't believe this shit; I usually have one woman, but today I have two freaks rubbing me down. You all are giving me the best happy ending of my life."

Meiying digs deep in his temple while Mei starts to slowly stroke his cock with oil. Heaven sent hands blesses his moans. Meiying kisses his earlobes and rubs his neck. He thrust his cock in the air, meeting Mei's hands as they keep gliding and rubbing his shaft. She blows on the tip of his head. His moans become louder as he grabs Meiying by her ass. He rubs and smacks it as his nut rises to the mushroom tip.

"Shāshāng," they shout in unison. Mei lets go of his shaft, jumps on his face, lifts up her skirt and the pastor quickly indulge in her pussy.

As he eats, Meiying pulls the blade out, walks to his dick and slices it. Blood and cum fly everywhere while Mei severs his throat with another blade.

Mei slices his dick off as a trophy. The mission is complete, and we laugh about this being the best kill ever. We make sure to wipe down all of the evidence and get dressed.

We leave the building unnoticed; but we would love to see the faces on the staff when the dickless pastor is found.

MALAKAI

I received a text message that it's finally over. I can't wait to see this on the evening news. I can see it already: Prominent Baptist Preacher Found Slaughtered in Local Massage Parlor.

I forget about the pastor and call Kryptonite about tonight's celebration. He's cool with meeting the twins at the club.

I'm enjoying the peace today, since Asperilla has been gone for 2 weeks and it's kind of lonely in the house without her.

I decided to jog down Bay Shore. That's the only place I can see a ton of women running half-naked. I believe in staying fit, not just to look good, but to stay healthy too. Okay, fuck that. I do it to look good.

The Shore is crawling with all different types of women. I'll even fuck one of those just-had-a-baby moms walking around here pushing a stroller. Hell yeah, I bet she still has milk in those titties. I laugh because I know I'm a damn fool.

I run fast, but there are some ladies here that can run really fast. I only come here to see how much ass I can pass.

I see two white girls running, and they are thick as hell. I couldn't see myself dating one, but I'll fuck the shit out of one. Well, in this case, maybe two.

I must be feeling extra good because I run by them and say that out loud without realizing it.

They both shoot me a grin back, and I know their pussies are saying, "Freak, come eat."

"Have a great day, ladies." They'll have men all over them by the end of their run.

I love this city; out here, the weather is almost perfect. The seagulls are looking for food, old men are fishing, and people are roller skating. I never had this type of atmosphere in Alabama; I was just a country bumpkin.

I'm so distracted by everything around me that I run into this fine-ass woman.

"Excuse me," I politely say.

"I didn't know poets enjoy running," she says.

"Do I know you?" I ask.

"Not really," she smiles, "I have seen you perform, and I would love for you to be a feature at Club Xpressionz?"

We exchange numbers.

She blushes and says, "My name is Love Divine."

"Baby, I love that name." For some reason, I don't see her as a fuck but as a woman that shares my vision.

We joked a little more, and I tell her I have to get back home before nightfall.

"Mommy doesn't let you stay out past the streetlights?" she laughs.

"I am my own man; I just have some business to handle."

I met a new poet, and I know, by the time I get home today, the news will be on full blast about the pastor's death.

I arrive home, and of course Asperilla opens the door buck naked with heels on, talking about, "it's dinner time."

We will fuck later but I'm not in the mood right now, because I know the 6:30 news will have everything I need to hear today.

"Asperilla, you haven't watched the news?" I ask.

"Hell naw, I am the news, and everyone knows I am the shit. It must be something really serious on TV today to make you pass up all of this pussy," she reveals.

I turned on the TV in the living room and it was everywhere.

"The body of one of Florida's biggest congregation leaders has been found in a local massage parlor. His throat was cut and inappropriate mutilations of his body," anchor reports.

Asperilla runs into the room screaming, "Malakai, you are evil as hell, but I love you."

I'll thank the twins later tonight.

Out the corner of my eye, I see Asperilla sliding one of her favorite toys in and out of her pussy. I know I'm a freaky muthafucker, but this bitch makes me think her pussy is like the black hole. I finish watching the news, drama is over, and my girls can relax. I tell Asperilla to go upstairs to get served.

You would have thought she trains with Usain Bolts, the way she sprints in heels.

My phone rings before I get to the stairs. It's Ayanna on the other end. She's laughing for a change.

"I guess the pastor got exactly what he deserved. I'm glad someone cut his damn dick off." She pauses. "Malakai, I have something to ask you. If I want to get out the business, will you be mad at me? I am thinking about moving back home to be with my family and to start a new life."

"Ayanna, you are one of my best workers, but I do understand. You already know the rule: you can leave as long as you bring me a new face."

"Good," she says in relief. "I've been searching for a woman that would be the money maker to make both of us retire from the game."

We laugh at the same time.

"You can start working on that deal," I tell her, "but slowly and carefully. Enjoy your evening, Ayanna."

As soon as I hang up the phone, Asperilla screams at me. "Malakai! Come and fuck me!"

This damn broad of mine.

I strip out of my clothes before I make it to the first step. I'm going to feed her this angry dick.

By the time I get in the room, I'm naked, and she's licking her lips with a bowl of juicy pineapple slices beside her.

"Don't think this fuck will excuse you of your behavior," I say.

"I knew you would like your favorite fruit," she says.

Laying them on her nipples and clit, "Come and eat, you sexy nigga," she passionately whispers.

I have my tongue ready and erect. Yeah, it takes a bad man to make his tongue hard. I'm about to eat 'til I throw up cum. Moments like this, I know why I fell for Asperilla; she knows how to unleash the beast in me. I love watching her glide those pineapples around her pussy.

I get on my knees and suck her toes while she grabs her nipples and moans, "Yes, baby, yes." I make sure to suck them slow, one by one, 'til she begs me to stop. Working my way up, slurping and sucking this tongue around her ankles and calves.

"Malakai, stop playing and make me cum!" she screams.

I jump on the bed and throw her legs back. Placing the pineapple on her clit, I lick around the pineapple and finger her pussy with short strokes. I use my tongue to kiss, twist and twirl her ass clean. She arches her back and throws that pussy in my face. Then, all of a sudden, she grabs my head and gets rough.

"Eat, nigga!"

This freak thinks she can drown me, but she has no idea that I live to suck cum holes dry. She fucks my face, and I love it. I come up for air.

"Harder, muthafucker," I shout.

She wraps her legs around my head and pumps my face.

"Yes, Malakai, I love you, Papi!" Her body shakes and shivers, and then she screams, "I'm about to cum!"

I refused to let her win, so I held on tight for this ride.

She squirts so much cum in my face that half of the shit goes in my damn nose. I love every minute of it. I love tasting her, and swallowing it is even better. She thinks she's going to rest, so I put this dick in her sweet spot and bite on her nipples and fuck her hard.

We make a mess in the bed; cum, pineapple juice, and more cum. We don't give a damn because we want to tame each other. I slow stroke that pussy for a minute, flip her over and make her ride backwards.

She gets on top and bounces on this dick, grabs her ankles and bounces harder.

I pump back, and we're sweating our asses off.

"Muthafucker, whose dick is this?" she moans "Say it! Say it!"

I play her game, slap her ass, and say, "It's Asperilla's dick!"

"Say it again, muthafucker!"

"It's Asperilla's dick!"

I know that makes her wild, but deep down it's my dick. No woman deserves to have my dick to claim as her own. She rides faster; I know it's time to shoot this nut, and she feels my body tense.

She flips around and sucks my dick like a hungry bum with free food. She's jacks my dick in her mouth. I unleash this flood and cum shoots down her throat. She doesn't say a word until she licks her lips.

"Thanks for the protein."

"THERE ARE SUPERHEROES, AND THERE ARE
MEN THAT CAN LAST FOREVER IN HER
WETNESS. DO YOU WANT A CAPE OR RATHER
BE AQUAMAN BETWEEN HER THIGHS?"

CHAPTER 13

MALAKAI

I jump up when I hear the doorbell, look at the clock, and it's only 10:30 pm.

"Oh shit, I am damn late, fucking around with Asperilla and those pineapples."

I must have kicked my phone off or something, but I have business to handle tonight. I threw on a pair of shorts, a tank and run downstairs. I usually don't have company, so I wonder who the hell is at my door. I open the door and it's Kryptonite standing there, all dressed and shit.

"Nigga, you're late," is all he says.

I hate being late for anything. Time is the only thing I have in this world, and I need to make the best of it every day.

"Yeah, I know, but give me about thirty minutes to shower and get dressed and we can roll out."

"Yeah, take care of your damn breath." He laughs. "Tell that woman that your mouth is not a flossing machine for her pussy. Your mouth smell like a porn set, cum juice everywhere."

"Real funny, man. Just give me a damn minute, and I'll be ready. Come on in and make yourself at home." I mention.

I can hear him laughing and talking about my mouth. I have no idea why he and Asperilla hate each other, but I have love for them, so I listen to both sides.

I run upstairs, turn the shower on, and wash quickly. Any other time I'd stay in here forever, but I have a late-night meeting. I make sure to brush my teeth, floss, and gargle with mouthwash. I know my mouth isn't that funky, but just in case. I have to be on top of my game.

I dress, kiss Asperilla, and run back downstairs.

We leave the house, and I have no idea whose car this dude has, but it's nice as hell. I'm staring at a Jaguar XF, and it's so clean that the moon is afraid to beam on it. He knows I'm feeling it.

We hit the interstate, pull up to Club AJA Channelside, and valet is ready to park this car. We entered the club and I love the scenery.

Mei and Meiying are on the dance floor, acting a damn fool. Those girls know how to party, and they're dancing all nasty up on each other. They do look sexy, but we have to close the loop.

They see us, leave the dance floor and head to the bar. They get their drinks, saying they love it here and might invest in a condo downtown. I politely watch them down their drinks. I don't have to ask them to leave; they're ready.

I heard Chris Brown is in town, and this will be the after-party spot. We need to leave before this place turns into a mad house.

The valet brings the car, and we go for a ride. The girls ask if they can go to the beach and watch the stars while we talk about how everything went.

It's hard to believe that I am gazing at stars when I just had a man murdered for fucking with my girls.

Mei does most of the talking since Meiying is tipsy. Mei is a smart chick, and she knows how to play the field.

She asks, "are you interested in visiting China to start an operation with us since we love how smooth your service runs in the states? There is serious money to make because they love cock."

"It really doesn't sound like a bad idea, and I'll get back with you at the end of the month. Anyway, how was the kill?" I inquire.

Mei smiles and shouts, "Oh, that was the shit! I still have his dick in my pocket."

"What the fuck!" I yell.

She laughs, "Hey, do you want to see it?"

"Bitch, hell naw," I scold. "Take that shit to China."

Mei smirks and sings, "I have a real dildo."

I swear this girl's sense of humor can cast her for comedy central.

We admire the view and discuss more about the overseas operation.

Meiying feels on herself and say, "I need to fuck!"

We talk business and take them back to their hotel. Mei kisses me and says thanks for the fast cash and let her know if she can take out another person.

I laugh. "I think I'm good for now but will make sure you're the first I hire."

Kryptonite jumps out of the car and tosses the keys. "Come and get me tomorrow morning. I am going to eat Chinese in a minute."

"Damn, dude, you fuck more than me." I say while pointing.

"And I bust more nuts than you," he says while winking at Mei.

I can't complain because if he isn't fucking, he's killing. I could have easily had him take care of the pastor, but even a killer needs a vacation. I watched them go into the hotel.

I'm cruising on the interstate, changing lanes, and enjoying my music zone until the police lights are flashing behind me. I know I could lose their ass, but it's too much damn trouble. I pulled to the side and waited.

I handed the cop my license.

I don't look until she speaks, "I've being following you since you left the hotel."

This bitch is fine.

I ask, "That's cool, but why did you pull me over?"

"It's not what you did," she says, "It's what you will be doing. My shift ends at 6:30 am; here's my number and address. I would love to talk about a possible business proposal that can save your life after a morning fuck."

She gives back my license, walks to her car and speeds off.

I guess Lil Wayne's not the only man that can fuck a cop. One day my dick might fall off because of pussy, but as long as this muthafucker rises, I will serve it hard and real.

I know I don't have long before the sun cracks the sky; the waffle house is the perfect place to waste time. The restaurant is packed, but I enjoy my omelet. I eat my last bite, call the officer, and ask if she's ready for her adventure.

I pull up to her house and she comes to the door, standing in boots, stockings, hat, and handcuffs. This woman is so damn sexy. I lick my lips and walk in the door.

"GOOD PUSSY SOMETIMES PULLS YOU OVER AND THROWS IT IN YOUR FACE. TO EAT OR NOT TO EAT; THAT IS THE QUESTION."

CHAPTER 14

MALAKAI

After a good morning fuck, the officer finally tells me her name is Melissa. I smile and tell her she can pull me over anytime she's horny. She says she'll keep that in mind the next time she sees me on the streets.

I leave to pick up Kryptonite and make sure he's still living after a night with the girls.

I arrive at the hotel, and they're outside laughing and having the time of their lives. Kryptonite tells them that he'll visit China next month to conduct business. They came to my car with serious looks on their faces.

"Malakai," Mei says, "you really should think about moving your services to the Far East."

I know they're good for business, but honestly, I have other things on my mind. I will keep my thoughts to myself for now.

Kryptonite gives the twins hugs, jumps in the car and say, "My mission here is done; you can take me to the airport."

"Man, the only thing you did was fuck the whole time you were here." I state.

"Damn right. And the next time you call me, I'll do it again."

I laugh and press the gas. "By the way, whose damn car is this?"

"It's a friend and as a matter of fact, you need to drop it off because I promised her some dick, with her thirsty ass." He remembers.

"Hell nah! She can pick it up from the airport. I can't call Asperilla and ask her to pick me up from some crazy bitch's house." I protest.

We laugh and listen to music. I tell him about the officer, her deep throating skills and how she loves to be handcuffed. He laughs.

I tell him, "She wanted to be fucked with a nightstick for foreplay."

"You and these crazy-ass broads," he says shaking his head.

"I love them to death. You just make sure you haven't got the Chinese clap for screwing those girls last night. You better make sure your dick is still attached. You know they like taking trophies home with them."

He grabs his dick. "All's well that fucks well." He switches subjects. "You should hit New York with me, and then head to Philly. Their spoken word venues are off the chain."

I say, "I'm looking for a new spot to chill, and my vacation is much needed."

"Just keep me posted. I'll have everything laid out for you. You know you wouldn't have to worry about nothing."

I pulled up to the airport terminal and helped him grab his bags. "I love you like a son, Malakai," he says seriously, "but remember to watch your back. I have been in the game for a minute, and money changes people."

I consider him the father I never had. I know he's always cared enough to keep me out of trouble, so when he speaks, I listen.

"See you next time, Malakai," he says as he waves good-bye.

I called Asperilla and told her to meet me at the mall. I'll be nice enough to leave old girl's car there as well.

When I got to the mall, I called the number Kryptonite gave me.

She's cussing and fussing over the phone, "Y'all niggas think cause y'all got some good dick, you can take a bitch's car and keep it until whenever?"

"Look, woman, I'm just doing a favor for a friend. Your car will be in the parking lot close to the front of Nordstrom."

She is still talking shit, so I simply give her the click. I put her keys under the mat and walked inside the mall.

I walked to Milano Exchange to look for something nice to wear for this evening. There are cuties everywhere. I keep my cool because I'm done for today.

My phone rings, and it's Love Divine, asking me if I can make it to the spot Saturday night. I tell her that I'll be there, hard cock and ready to rock.

"You are so damn silly," she says, "and thanks for coming." We disconnected, and I kept on moving through the mall.

I keep shopping, and two hours pass. Asperilla is either late or up to no good with Pandora's crazy ass. I love this mall, and the nightclub outside would make a beautiful spot to have a spoken word event. I walk until I make it to a women's store and flirt with a few ladies.

My phone rings before I enter the store, and it's Asperilla telling me she's pulling up in less than five.

Well, I guess it'll have to be another time to flirt with the ladies. I make it outside, and she's smiling from ear to ear.

She explains, "I found this perfect dress but wasn't leaving the store 'til all the alterations were made."

I should have known. I get in on the passenger side, tongue her down, and we drive off.

She smiles at me, "How was the night? Or should I say the morning?"

"Everything went according to plan." I smiled back.

She keeps driving, saying she'd like to know if I'll ride to a new club in Clearwater.

"That sounds wonderful," I tell her, "especially after I get some sleep."

We pulled up into the driveway, and she's still talking about this new spot. I ask if Pandora is coming, and she's like, "You know it."

I shake my head and laugh; I know she'll be wild and off the wall tonight. I better get some rest because I'm going to need it.

ASPERILLA

"Bitch! You work for me, and when I tell you I want my money, then you will have my motherfuckin' money."

This stupid hoe got one more time to keep bringing up Malakai's name, like he has anything to do with my extra hoes on the side. He's always treating these bitches like royalty. This bitch is still yacking on the phone about how she's tired, wants to sleep and refuses to fuck on her period. I tell her to open her mouth or take it up the ass, but I want my damn money. I hang up on her retarded ass.

I'll check on that stupid bitch in a few days. I should have sung the chorus to *Stupid Hoe* from Nicki Minaj. They don't want Malakai to know I posted their bail, so they've been doing extra tricks for me. I'll ride this damn train as long as I can, and when that muthafucker goes on vacation, I will turn his business out.

I know he doesn't trust me; shit, I don't even trust my own damn self at times. I'm going to have a team full of hoes working for me, and I might even get some men to slang dick on the side; that sounds good as hell.

I laugh to myself and my thoughts shift back to the club; I'm going to let it all out tonight. When I throw on my heels and the tightest dress I own, it's to make every man in the club want to fuck me, but I'll be thinking about fucking their women.

I love my bisexual side; it's one of the greatest feelings to lick and stick. Damn, I need to open up a sex store with that name. I make a mental note of that.

I go upstairs and search through my closet. Malakai is in the hot tub soaking. I leave him alone for now, but he better be ready tonight to dick me and Pandora down. This will be our first outing, and I'm ready for her to share our bed.

I turn the radio on and twerk in the mirror. I could have been a dancer, because I have all the right moves and a body from heaven. I dance to the safe, hit the combination, grab some cash, and make it rain on myself. When you got the money I have, you can do that all the time.

I'll buy the bar out tonight, and the VIP room will be explosive. I stop daydreaming to get my outfit together. I call Pandora, and she sounds so damn good until I'm ready to taste the words rolling off her tongue. We laugh, talk shit, and get ready to make this a night to remember.

I find my shoes that will kill this dress, and no underwear will be worn, not even a thong. My pussy will speak its own language when I walk in that bitch.

I continue dancing in the mirror and make my ass clap. When I look up again, Malakai is standing there with a towel around his waist; water dripping down his chest. There's no telling how long he's been watching. I drop down into a split and bounce my ass cheeks to the beat. Yeah, nigga, I am the shit.

CHAPTER 15

MALAKAI

After watching Asperilla bounce her ass, I'm a little anxious about going to the club with these freaks. She asks me if I like what I see.

I just laugh and walk out of the room.

She shouts down the hall, "Give me about two hours, and I'll be ready to tear the club up."

"Fine," I shout. I jump into my poetic alter-ego and think of things to spit at the venue Saturday.

Tonight, my spit is out on parole,
So, fasten your seatbelt and hold onto your soul.
Watch how I lick, kiss, and tongue twist a metaphor
'til you forget that it even exists.
Watch how I seduce these words and verbs to death.
Leave them like I do my woman.
AHHHH, Gasping for Breath.

I'm feeling that shit; I'll finish it tomorrow. I lay my clothes out for the evening with precision because I'm going to enjoy myself. I get dressed, go downstairs, and make a drink. I watch one of my action movies and chill 'til Asperilla walks downstairs. I love some damn Bruce Lee, especially when he decides to whoop Chuck Norris's ass.

I'm all into it, and then I hear Asperilla speaking Spanish upstairs. She does that a lot lately. I guess she thinks I'm an average Joe, but I know more words than she gives me credit for. She walks down as stunning as the moonlight on a clear night.

We decided to roll in the Escalade and pick up Pandora.

We arrive at her house, and she has excellent taste, but she's as money hungry as Asperilla. She has the finest things, and, for a woman with no man, she holds her own.

We pull up at Club Ultimate; it's packed. There are so many delightful ladies. We walk in, and I see a few fellas I know from around the way and some that want to get at my girls. We sit in the VIP section, and a few of my girls are already there. I guess they made enough money and ended their shift.

I'm getting my drink on while Asperilla and Pandora grind on each other on the dance floor. This will be a great night.

I talked to a few of the girls, and everything is going well.

They played some throwback songs, and then I heard *Planet Rock*. I almost bust a nut. That will always be my shit.

The whole place erupts, and everyone is dancing while bubbles flow from the ceiling. People are breakdancing, ticking, and popping. I go old-school and hit the prep on their asses. Pandora and Asperilla come up and sandwich me; they're drunk as hell, talking about how they want to fuck me tonight. I know this is going to be one hell of a night, but I'm down for the adventure. I've never shared a woman with Asperilla, but I've always wanted to fuck Pandora.

I guess you can call me a poetic whore because I love fucking. I'll eventually settle down, but right now I have to make up for all the pussy I didn't get when I was wet behind the ears. Like the old folks used to say: Young, dumb, and full of cum. I am full of it, too, and tonight it will get released on asses, faces, and titties.

We are partying and celebrating like it's New Year's Eve.

I finally sat down and pull one of the girls to the side. "We're having a meeting real soon, and it's very important that you all are there."

She says, "No problem. I'll have the ladies there naked and standing at attention," she says as she sips her drink.

I laugh. "Not this time; it won't be that type of meeting. No search."

We part ways, and I decide to go enjoy my beautiful night of pleasure with two of the freakiest bitches on the planet.

We head home, and they are drunk and horny; a lethal combination and I know it's time for me to slay their asses. We arrive at the house, and they run like it's a damn race. I slowly step inside the door, and they're stripping out of their clothes, throwing panties, titties swinging like savage beasts in the jungle.

I decided to watch them feast on each other. Before I get too comfortable, I grab a man's best friend; yeah, my damn pussy sleeve.

"Hell yeah, let's get ready to rumble!" I shout while running to get my toy. I've got the one with the ripples flowing through the inside; the more you clean it, the better it feels.

They're fingering and licking each other's pussy, and I'm rock hard. I spit on my dick and stroke it a few times before I slide the sleeve on; moving my hands up and down while watching the show. Pandora's titties are so damn perfect. I know Asperilla is watching, and she wants to let Pandora know who runs shit so she orders her around.

I stand up, and Pandora crawls to me. Slowly pumping a few more strokes in my sleeve, I kiss it, and tell my baby I'll catch her another time.

Pandora sucks my balls smoothly while Asperilla eats her ass. She has a tongue that could get a brother hooked. She flicks it 'til she reaches my head, licks and kisses it. Yes, baby. I guess she loves getting her ass eaten because it doesn't faze her at all; she's determined to swallow this dick. She opens her mouth like a human anaconda.

She dives on my dick, and all I hear is the slushing of her mouth, no bullshit. Pandora is a headmaster; like the drive thru car wash, she's rinsing this dick. Grabbing the back of my ass, forcing me to throw it down her throat. Hell yeah, I am loving this.

Asperilla shouts, "Suck his brains off!"

I'm in no mood to hold this nut tonight so I grab her by the hair and fuck her mouth; pumping a few times until I explode. I push her on the ground and start to eat her pussy the same way she gave me head: ruthless and uncut! I go at that pussy like a dog fight, sucking like a fucking whirlwind, picking her up and let her straddle my face.

Asperilla picks up where Pandora left off and sucks my dick.

Pandora is a trooper, talking shit and screaming my damn name.

The more she screams, the more Asperilla sucks.

Pandora grabs the back of my head and fucks my face. I love it when a woman takes control while she's on top. She cums down my face, and the taste is so damn scrumptious. I push Pandora off my face and tell Asperilla to stop sucking my dick. I command her to lie down and let Pandora eat that pussy while I ram this dick in from behind. I tell Pandora that I'm going to push her face out of Asperilla's pussy by the time I bust this nut in her ass.

I let those freaks get real comfortable. I spit on my dick and wipe it down real good, use my fingers to tickle Pandora's clit. She lets out a small moan.

"Daddy, I am going in." She doesn't waste another minute to start cleaning Asperilla's black hole.

I jump in that pussy like a bench rider entering the game for the first time. I smack that ass every time my dick slides in and out. We're burning friction tonight.

I'm dancing in Pandora's wet pussy, and it farts with every damn stroke.

Asperilla grabs her hair and fucks her face hard, yelling, "Bitch! Don't stop 'til I squirt this nut all over you. I love the view from here. We're fucking hard, strong, and long until one of us passes out."

Pandora is moaning and groaning.

Asperilla shouts, "Yeah, you like Malakai dick! I know you do!"

I keep banging that ass like I'm shooting off a rocket from the Kennedy Space Center. Asperilla's face starts to change colors; that means she's about to squirt. She pushes Pandora's face back and fingers her clit faster than the speed of light.

Asperilla screams, "Get your fucking face down here and catch this squirt!" I push her head back down, and she skeets like a garden hose all over Pandora's face. I wait 'til she finishes wetting her ass up before I jump out the pussy and begin to jack my dick over their faces.

I ask, "Who wants this nut?"

They scream, "Feed me!" as I spray their asses with the death blow. Releasing my energy, and I feel like a muthafucking king. I am enjoying this damn pleasure, and I can feel chills down to my very soul every time I think of that damn word. I just think my mind is playing tricks on me.

I lie down knowing it's going to happen again, but for this one moment, I want to have the joy of two beautiful ladies resting their heads on my chest.

CHAPTER 16

MALAKAI

Last night was one hell of an encounter. Asperilla and Pandora are still lying naked when I get up. I'd say they are made for each other. I swear, Pandora must have fallen asleep between Asperilla's legs, because her face is still there. I laughed and hit the shower.

I have to check on the girls today and get in touch with Love Divine for the rundown on Saturday's show.

I stay in the shower a little longer than usual, but when I get out Pandora is standing in my face.

"You know," I say, "there is more than one bathroom in this house."

"I know, but I just wanted to see what you look like fresh out the shower."

I give her a *whatever* grin and walk away.

She slaps my ass. "You have a beautiful ass for a nigga."

In my mind, I make a mental note to never be left alone with that freak; she might try to shove dildos in my ass or something.

I get dressed, eat, and tell the ladies I'll be home later. It's not like they really cared or anything; they'll probably just sex each other senseless.

I called Love Divine to get the information on the show. She answers in a sexy voice.

"This is Malakai," I say.

She laughs. "I have caller ID, fool."

"Is the show still on for this weekend?" I asked, laughing.

"I was giving you time to wake up," she says, "but the show won't happen this Saturday. I have something better for you. Since you haven't been to Texas, I booked a gig for you next week."

"For real?" I'm smiling like a little kid in a candy store.

She states, "Yeah, we can meet in Houston and perform a piece together. Don't mess it up."

I laugh and say, "I'll be ready and on fiyah."

She thanks me and appreciates the love.

We hung up and I decided to go to the bank to do a quick rundown on my accounts. I always have money hidden in the Cayman Islands and Swiss accounts.

While flirting with the manager, she informs me of the large transfer with my account lately.

This is the account I share with Asperilla and don't understand why she would transfer $50,000 without my knowledge, but I'll get to the bottom. First, it was the preacher, now the money; that's two strikes. Her ass is almost out the door.

I thanked her and asked her to please call me the next time a transfer happens and she agrees to keep me posted on all of the accounts. This information has me with a new mindset.

I call the only escort I can trust. She answers on the first ring, and that's what I love about Ayanna: she's true to her calling. I asked her to meet me in Ybor City today, and she agrees. I have to run my business proposal by her; I know she wants to get out of the game, but I can count on her to do one last favor when I hit the ground in Houston. I'm planning to set up shop and maybe even invest in a little club spot as well. Ayanna is pretty excited to be a part of the setup. She tells me that she knows the perfect girl to stir up the city. When she leaves, I will truly miss her. We set the time and hung up.

I met Ayanna five years ago working at a restaurant. I knew she had all the right tools on the first night. She saw my ride and asked if I was into the drug game. I smiled and said, "Nah, just pussy."

She laughed. "That is the wildest shit I ever heard."

We talked all night, and, by the end, she was ready to do whatever. Now she has the whole city on lock, and if she ever wanted to do it on the side and become a Madam, I wouldn't be mad at her at all.

I need to do something to waste time 'til I meet Ayanna. I decided to go to the dollar movie theatre, which is something I haven't done in a long time.

Plenty of old movies playing, but I will watch The Vow.

I called Asperilla after the movie, but she didn't answer. Probably using toys with Pandora. I rode to Saint Pete to meditate on the pier.

For some reason, I give my attention to God.

I say my prayers with spoken word because I feel that is my connection back to my Maker.

Heavenly Father, I know my sins outweigh the good.
I need to do better and I should.
It is not even the money or the fame.

You told me if I don't change,

Heaven will erase my name.

I am out here misusing the Queens of the earth.

I am so wrong for not telling them

What they are really worth.

I should give this away

And become the poet that You created me to be.

As I watch what you created, it is so beautiful;

Is this how heaven's going to be?

Change starts within,

And I am really going to focus

On putting away these sins.

Lord, I thank You for another blessing

Even through my corrupted life.

You always make a way.

I just thank you for allowing me to see another day. Amen!

I finished my prayer and my phone rings. Ayanna asks if I'm ready to meet her at the spot. I'm truly motivated to leave this life behind. I'll do this last run in Houston, and, after that, I'm calling it quits to focus on spoken word and my clubs.

I meet Ayanna at a Cuban restaurant; I love sitting outside watching all the people pass by. You never know what you'll see in Ybor. I once saw a dude dressed like an angel, passing out Bible tracts in the middle of the road. I joked and asked if he was

Michael, and he was like, "My name is Ralph." I fell out laughing, but I did commend him for being bold enough to walk Ybor.

Everything happens in this part of Tampa. I order my drinks and tell the waiter to check back in five. Ayanna walks up, and she's not alone. She has one of the finest black chicks I have ever seen with her. I let out a sly grin and got up. I pull the chairs out for the lovely ladies. I can't even get a word out before Ayanna says, "Malakai, this is Jazmine, and she's from Houston."

I say, "Ayanna, you are going out with a bang. I just told you about the Houston deal and you already have things lined up."

"You can thank me with a bonus," she says. "Jaz is a long way from home and new to the city but very ambitious. I didn't want her working the streets of Tampa. She's done a few parties with old men that wouldn't take advantage of her. But it gave her a chance to gain some experience."

"Well done, Ayanna. It's a damn shame you are retiring soon. I could use your expertise," Malakai says.

Ayanna smiles and says, "Before I leave the game, everything will be set and ready for takeover. Jaz is a little shy, but after a few drinks she makes Sasha Fierce look normal."

"Jaz, please stand up so I can look at you. Indeed, you are a goldmine." We talk for a while, and guys are staring at us all night.

Ayanna tells Jaz that if she can make that dude buy our drinks, she'll give her a grand just for fun.

I want to see this. Only a fool would buy drinks for another man while he chills with the ladies.

Jaz doesn't waste any time, and I'm eager for her skills to be displayed. She walks over, grabs him by the shirt, and puts her ankle on his shoulder. She doesn't even lose her balance.

I bet that dude's got an eyeful of pussy. Jaz moved like a kick boxer or something.

She whispers in his ear and starts to spit her game.

Ayanna quickly catches my attention and brings me to reality saying, "Asperilla is full of shit sometimes and it's her fault Cherry was caught up with the pastor."

I will talk to that ass tonight. Damn, Asperilla's name is in too much shit.

I console her saying, "Tell Cherry, I won't rest until her attacker is dead."

I glance back at Jaz, and she's twisting her hips with his debit card and cash in hand.

"I don't know what the hell she said to that man, but, damn, I got a hustler on my team. Hell, yeah! H-Town is about to knock some boots once again," I say proudly.

We pay for the drinks with his card, and Jaz gives him her number. I hug and kiss them on the cheek, walk them to their car, tell Jaz she is the truth and I can't wait to see her in full moon potential.

She laughs and says, "Malakai, I promise I won't let you down."

They drive off as I walk down the street when I hear my name. The voice is so familiar that all I can do is smile. It's the First Lady, and I'm like, what the hell is she doing down in Ybor City?

She gives me a big hug and smile, but I'm so surprised that I froze in my tracks for a moment. I can tell she's hanging out with a few of her friends; something different for women's fellowship.

I let her talk, "I have become the fulltime pastor at the church. The world needs to see someone that can stand despite all circumstances. Having sex with you was wrong, I admit but I was of the flesh and my sins have been forgiven. I must continue to save lost souls and restore the image of my husband's legacy."

"All temptation and seduction are gone and I wish you the best in your ministry," I respond with concern.

She smiles and says, "We will meet again, Malakai; I can assure you of that."

I know that she's a blessing, as I give her a kiss and hug that would last a lifetime.

She turns her attention to her friends, and they disappear down the street.

I rode through the city with normal speed praying my friendly officer pulls me over. Chills of pleasure running down my soul; I truly can't stop asking for more of it.

I need to work on this duet with Love Divine, because our piece will be fiyah when we perform.

I am enjoying my life, but I can't do this forever. I called my sister because we haven't spoken since my last visit. She answers on the second ring.

"You still living? I haven't heard from your ass in three months," she fusses.

"I've been a little busy, but I promise I'll visit Alabama once I start the movement in Houston," I confess.

"Whatever, just bring me a few lottery tickets," she laughs.

My sister and I had a rough life, but, with her keen mind for the streets, she always made a way. We joke and reminisce about the good old days. I will make the arrangements for her to visit so she can enjoy herself, but I tell her to act like she has some sense this time and keep that damn weed at home; she's the best in my eyes, and I tell her that we'll see each other soon.

As I hung up the phone, I hit a quick left and went to the spot to see what's popping. I'll let my sexy officer be free tonight. I want to stop by *Poetic Heaven* to see what the vibe is like tonight. I run my business to the T. Even though I'm not there all the time, the money comes in hard, so I just review the papers and help with the ideas. I have a partner to assist when I'm not able to attend.

I walk through, making sure things are going smoothly and greet everyone for happy hour. I shout to the bartender that the next round is on me as I walk out the door.

Picking up my cell, "Asperilla, we need to have a serious talk."

"We sure do, Papi," she whispers, "and my ears will be wider than my pussy."

"Look, I am not in a joking mood. Just have your ass available when I get home," I scorn.

"Yes sir," she sadly says as she hangs up.

"ONE OF THE BIGGEST REGRETS IN LIFE IS
BREAKING IT OFF WITH SOMEONE BEFORE
YOU FUCK THEM ONE LAST TIME."

CHAPTER 17

MALAKAI

As soon as I open my front door, Asperilla is sitting in a chair in the middle of the floor. I think to myself *this bitch is crazy,* but I just leave it alone.

"I see you are ready for our conversation?" I ask.

"Yeah, and I can't wait to hear what you got to say, since you sounded serious and shit," she replies.

"It is," I say, "so, if you don't mind, please stop making me feel uncomfortable and have a seat on the loveseat or something."

She gets up and clicks her heels like she's Dorothy in The Wizard of Oz or something.

I laugh, and it's times like these that make me think of all the fun we had. But business comes first tonight. "Asperilla, I'm heading to Houston next week to do a show and network with some more investors. I'll be home Sunday. I need you to hold it down and make sure the ladies are supplied with whatever is needed for success."

"Malakai, I have been around hoes all my life; you keep forgetting it was my idea in the first place," she barks.

"Yep, it was your idea, but it was also your ideas that almost got us put behind bars three years ago." I say reminiscing.

"Damn," she yells, "can you just let the past go and move the fuck on?"

A sly grin comes across my face as I whisper in her ear, "I will never forget." I pulled away. "I love you, Asperilla, but if you ever pull another stupid ass stunt like the preacher incident, I'm leaving your ass without return."

She mumbles under her breath and starts speaking Spanish like I can't understand shit.

I finish her sentence in Spanish and we say, "Ponme a prueba!"

The look she gives me, as if she sees a ghost and, for the first time, her ass is speechless.

I say," I know about the damn transfer so whatever the fuck you have planned ends now. Stop being an asshole to Cherry and the rest of the ladies. I love you to death but you can be happy with me or pack your shit tonight. Better yet, the money you have been taking, use that to photo shop you a new damn life."

She quickly jumps on the defensive side, and her accent becomes harder and stronger. "Fuck you, Malakai! You didn't build this empire by your damn self, and I have a right to the money just like you do!"

"Whatever, Asperilla. I don't want to fight. You have enough money in your account to do whatever. This conversation is over, and I don't want to discuss it again. I agree we have a great thing going, but I mean what I said: I am not cleaning up after your ass again. I'm flying out to Houston on Wednesday, and when I return, you can either behave or your ass will be in a grave. That's a poetic quote you can keep," I boast.

She bounces her ass from the sofa, "Kiss it, muthafucker," she says as she walks away.

I know she hates that I let the girls have leeway, and she wants to treat them like shit, but I'll say it again: these ladies don't sell just pussy, they sell a lifetime of memories.

I call Love Divine, and as soon as she says hello, my soul melts. That woman has a voice from heaven, and she knows it. I tell her that I'll be out there on Wednesday and we can rehearse a little before Saturday night's show. She agrees and says that she can't wait to see me.

I hang up the phone, strip out of my clothes, and head toward the shower. I pass by the bedroom and Asperilla flips me the bird. She's not upset; this is her crazy way of telling me that she wants some dick. I just pause for a second and blow her a kiss.

"Fuck you!" she yells.

"Fuck you!" I laugh and keep it moving.

After this shower, I'm heading to bed. I'm relaxing and thinking of my plans for Houston, then I realize Asperilla's, buck-ass naked, standing in front of me.

"Papi," she moans, "you know that you turn me on when you put me in my place. I love when you take control and make me surrender to you. I need this dick, and I want it right now."

She slowly drops down to her knees in the shower and licks the tip of my dick. Her tongue has a way of tickling my head 'til I want to beg her to stop. That damn shit always turns me on. I know I have to serve her, but, just for a moment, I lean back and let her deep throat my dick nice and slow. I grab her hair and slowly fuck her mouth. I twist my fingers through her hair while she grabs my ass and pushes me into her mouth with a smooth, quick force.

She moans and I look down and see the spit oozing out of the corner of her mouth. That is so sexy, and it doesn't stop her from swallowing this head. She hits that extra tempo, and you'd think she has hydraulics in the back of her neck, the way she's bouncing up and down on my dick. I've played with this feeling long enough. I squeeze my ass to hold the pressure. I release and dig into her throat, hitting the corners like balls on the pool table. I let go her hair, grab the back of her head and fuck her face.

I'm breathing hard, and she's in the zone. I think I catch a cramp in my stomach when I shoot that nut. When you bust a nut like that, you've got to take a break. I enjoyed that ride.

Asperilla wipes her mouth. "Papi, did I make up for doing wrong?"

I smile. "For now, yes, baby."

I dive in hard and lick that pussy with magnificent strokes of lightning on the bathroom floor.

"Eat this pussy, baby," she says, "I love when you put your nose in it."

I love her accent, and it makes me dig deeper. She digs her nails in my back, I let out a small yell, since I feel blood dripping. I love when she gets rough, and this is awesome.

I see her exhale, and I'm ready to catch all of her juices. I have my tongue so deep in her that her clit is tickling my tonsils. She's squeezing her muscles on my tongue, and I can sense she's about to cum. She bucks her last buck, and out it comes, flowing out like a volcano. And just like Pac-man, I gobble up all of her ghosts.

I raise up and press her face against the wall.

She reaches back, grabs my balls and screams, "Fuck me hard, Papi, and don't stop 'til I cum all down that dick."

I know she wants pain, and I'm going to try and rip up her insides. I run up in that pussy like a track star, with one hand mushing her face into the wall while the other one plays with her clit. I'm fucking and sweating. I refuse to stop; refuse to give in until I fulfill her wish.

Her pussy makes swishing sounds. She's throwing that pussy back, clenching my dick with every throw. I let go of her head and grab her waist and pull her onto my dick while I ram her shit. I go faster and harder with each stroke.

She's moaning and screaming. "I love this dick! I will kill you if you leave me!"

I hear her, but I'm so busy thinking about the pussy that it doesn't register that this woman just said she would kill me.

I keep drilling her ass out 'til she squirts. It's like clockwork because, as soon as she cums, I pull out and bust my load on her back. She enjoys every minute and then tells me to put it in her ass and bust one in there too.

Her asshole was never tight, but, like a slave, I do as she commands and fuck her hard in the ass as well. I keep the tempo strong 'til I release another missile into her spot. We exhale and come back to earth. We get into the shower, wash each other, dry off and head to bed.

CHAPTER 18

ASPERILLA

Pandora needs to hurry the hell up, because I am ready to hit the stores before I head to my dance class. She takes her sweet time, so I lay on the horn for about two minutes until her neighbors come running outside. I release the horn.

"What the fuck are ya'll looking at?" I yell, then go right back to blowing it. I begin to play the Too Short beat on the car horn until she finally comes outside.

"Asperilla, you are always somewhere acting a damn fool. You are going to have them call the police on me for disturbing the peace."

"Well, if you would have been on time, I wouldn't be acting like a monkey. Anyway, I really need this new Chanel purse to go with my heels for the next time we are out, and after that, we can go the Cheesecake Factory for lunch."

She quickly says yes; only because she knows I never go anywhere without buying her something nice as well.

We pull up to the mall, and, of course, the place is crowded. But my days of shopping at Old Navy are a thing of the past, because pussy is power. Every time one of those trick hoes spreads their legs, I am counting bread. We ran into Nordstrom so I can pick up my purse and try on a few clothes, but I'm not too impressed with the selections today.

"We should fly to New York," I say, "while Malakai is out in Houston."

"I'll travel to the moon with you as long as they have sexy heels," she says while batting her eyes.

I laugh, "You are so damn silly. I love that it is never a dull moment when we are together."

I paid for the purse and walked to Helzberg Diamonds to try on the earrings that grabbed my attention last week.

I waltz over and ask the salesclerk, "Could I please try on the diamond and emerald three-quarter carat earrings?" The saleswoman was delighted to show them, praying that she could get a sale off me.

She tells me the background of the earrings, price and slides me a credit application.

I am in a decent mood today; hopefully I won't have to emotionally fuck up her day.

I really dislike it when people assume that if you are not part of a certain society, then you don't have any money. I keep smiling and try on my earrings.

I tell her that they will be perfect with my dress for next weekend. I slowly take them off.

"The earrings are $2,299. We can still help you with a credit application and once approved, you can take them home," the saleswoman says.

Pandora looks at me. "Asperilla, please don't do it."

I say while handing her $2,500, "That will not be necessary, you can gift wrap them now and keep the change, bitch."

Pandora laughs in her face, and the white woman's face turns redder than a tomato.

Well, at least I didn't slap her face off for treating me like shit. The saleswoman walks back with my earrings gift-wrapped, "Thanks for shopping at Helzberg Diamonds."

We left the jewelry store, headed to the Cheesecake Factory to enjoy our beautiful lunch. The hostess seats us and tells us our waitress will be here shortly.

"Don't take this the wrong way but when are we going to fuck Malakai again," Pandora says.

Thinking to myself, *I doubt I will share my dick again. I have always been faithful to that fucka, at least with men, anyways.*

"Pandora, I'm not sure when the next round will be, because Malakai is on some bullshit right now," I tell her.

"When he stops tripping, keep me in the loop. Your man has an ass to die for."

I was about to say something out of line when the waitress came.

"Good afternoon, my name is Jacquise, and I will be your server today. May I start you two off with something to drink?"

Pandora orders the Firefly, while I ask for the Pomegranate Margarita.

The waitress says thank you and informs us that she will be right back with our drinks.

"Did you hear about that preacher that was killed at the massage parlor?" Pandora asks me. "That is truly some fucked up shit. I heard that his dick is still missing. That is some wild ass shit. I better watch myself when I am getting a pedicure,"

"Girl," I say, "you are so damn crazy. There is nothing that is going to happen to you while you are getting your toes done. Honestly, I think the fool got what he deserved. I really don't understand what pastor in his right mind would have sex in a massage parlor in broad daylight. Damn, have some sense to go at night."

The waitress comes back with our drinks, and we place our order as we continue our conversation.

I could tell her the truth, but some secrets need to be kept. "Pandora, would you like to come out to the next ballroom recital?" I ask.

"Yeah girl, I'll go--especially if those sexy dudes like the ones on Dancing with the Stars are there."

"You really need a social life. I swear to God you do," I smile.

She smiles back. "Yes, because working is killing me, so whatever excitement you throw my way, I am on it. I really do miss my days on the stripper pole, and if I wasn't known at the hospital, I would do it every other Friday just for fun."

"You need to sit your ass down somewhere, because we both know those days are over," I tell her.

"Yeah, you might be right, but I can still shake my ass with any of these non-talented hoes in this city."

The food comes at the right time, and we enjoy our delicious lunch. We laugh and bring up old memories until tears start to roll down from my eyes. Pandora burst out that she wants to have a baby.

I almost spit out my drink when she says that foolishness. "Asperilla, I am telling the truth." She says, "I will make a wonderful mother and a fantastic wife."

We leave the restaurant, and we're about to walk out of the door when these guys interrupt our time.

"Excuse me, Miss. My name is Hydro and I've seen you at a few spoken word spots in the city."

"If you have seen me around, then you should have asked my name when you saw me," I replied.

He looks startled and speechless.

"Does the cat have your tongue or just pussy? Because the last time I checked, if you see a lovely woman then you should speak. My name is Asperilla and this is Pandora. You have two minutes to spark my interest. Go!" I demand.

"Listen, I'm Hydro and I am a poet out of Orlando, and I would love to invite you and your friend out for a night of poetry. We are having poets from across the state to bless the mic. It would be an honor to have you at the show," he tells me.

"Wow," I say, "another fucking poet. I am going to level with you Hydro, Water boy, or Mr. H20. I have one poet in my life, and that fool is a headache and a walking asshole. I only go to shows to support him because I could care less about poetry. I stay to myself while he performs, but I am tied to Malakai."

His partners laugh like I'm a comedian or something.

Hydro says, "Asperilla, no disrespect, but I have been praying for that dude to come to one of my shows. I want to prove to him that he is not the only poet that can make a woman cream. If you can get him there, I bet that the ladies will love me more than him. I will give him love, but he's not ready for me and my clique. We go by the name of Soulful Stimulation and we're about to take over the movement of Nightlife and Poetry."

I know Malakai told me to behave but fuck that. I just had to hit the record button on my cell phone because he would not believe this shit with just my words.

I say boldly, "I will get him there, and you don't have to pay no feature fee or nothing. If he busts your little crew's asses, I want the money from the door, and you have to get on stage and write a poem about how you like to walk around in ladies panties."

Mr. Hydro wasn't laughing at all right now, but he had a serious look on his face.

He sticks his chest out and speaks. "If I win, then you owe me head for a week, ass the following week, and pussy for a month."

"Well, if that is the case then pull your dick out," I say.

He has nothing to say and no dick to produce. There goes an ego down the drain.

"Look, if you could possibly win this little erotic challenge then Pandora and I will fuck your brains out and give you $5,000, just for fun," I say laughing.

"Challenge accepted and the show is this Saturday and if he is a no-show, then I want my money and your ass," Hydro says.

"Will there be VIP plus a full house so I can watch your ass cry comfortably?" I asked with sarcasm.

"Yes, it will be packed to the wall and may the best poem win," he says as he walks away laughing.

Malakai should make me his fucking manager for all the things I be setting up.

Pandora looks at me. "Are you sure Malakai is up for this? He barely performs like he did back in the day."

I responded, "Trust me, that poetic whore lives and breathes this. He better do it. I'd hate to slice that other poet up, because I'll be damned if I suck anything that he pulls out. I should have followed them to their car. They might be riding in a damn mini-van or something."

We get on the highway because we still have to make it to the dance class. I can't be late. Arthur Murray Studios will charge whether you are there or not. Lord knows, I love to salsa and maybe I will attend one of their ballroom showcases and dance the night away.

Wow, I can't believe how fast the day went, but we had a bodacious time with shopping and the dance class. I drop Pandora off at home, pull up to our gate right before sunset. Instead of going into the house, I just stand on the porch and think about my life, things Pandora said about a baby and being a mother.

My past was hell, and my mother was fucking horrible, but I love her with all my heart. I put my face in my hands and let out some tears that have built up in me for many years. I have a chance to live a beautiful life with Malakai; we have more fortune than we can imagine.

We might have built these clubs on the backs and stomachs of escorts, but we aren't starving anymore.

As I place my key in the door, I hear the music playing upstairs and my heart skips a beat. I know some of ya'll are thinking it is about to be a romantic evening for me. Well, not even close, because that man of mine is upstairs performing poetry in the mirror butt-ass naked.

Oh, we will fuck tonight, but I'll allow him to fuck those words first. This is the perfect night to sell his ass to Orlando, so he can turn out the show.

I walk in the room as I watch him slowly spit out words and suck them back in. I wish his ass would have taken my advice and become a stripper or a poetic porn star. We could have taken the industry by storm with his chiseled chest, that juicy ass, and brown skin.

Shit! Just looking at him grinding is causing my juices to leak out three holes at the same time. I am wiping my mouth with one hand and my legs with the other one. He is going to sip all of this tonight.

"Malakai!"

He turns around with his dick in his hand. He begins to let the lyrical beast out.

If God created the world and said rest,

Then I want to create a universe with your black hole

And search through your milky way.

My tongue to become lost in your rings of Saturn

As I circle around your Venus.

Float into your deepest space

Until my mind becomes weak and erased.

Welcome home, baby,

Or shall I say Welcome to Space Age Freaking.

This damn dude is the reason why I keep panty liners in business.

He picks me up off the ground and whispers. "Do you want this dick or tongue first?" He slowly licks my earlobe. I want it so bad, but I need to close this deal.

"Yes Papi," I moan. He lays me on the bed, slides my dress off, and pulls off my lace panties with his teeth.

He places his face between my legs and tickles my clit with his nose. *Damn you, bastard.* I had to think real quick before I gave in and it's too late.

He begins to lap my juices like the dog he is, but he would add some finesse as well.

"Malakai, there is a spoken word event in Orlando." He just kept licking and moaning.

"I met a poet and he want to battle you; his name is Hydro."

He stops, slides off the bed and say. "Repeat that shit."

"His name is Hydro," I say, "and he's having an erotic show, and he wants you to battle his crew."

Malakai looks in my eyes. "Tell that fucka I'm there." He flips me on my stomach and starts to bite on my cheeks.

I am puzzled why the hell his ass didn't ask a zillion questions. There must be more to this story, and I will find out.

Until then, I'll get on all fours and take this steel tongue.

He licks my ass and moans. "I spit hot shit because I taste hot shit." I can tell I have pissed him off, because he is tongue fucking me fast as hell. He inserts one finger, then two and I twist my hips on top of them.

"Papi!" I moan faster as he fucks me, inserting one more finger into my walls. I can feel him cupping his way to my G-spot, and in a minute, I will flood his face with a tidal wave.

"You want this squirt?" I shouted. "Work for this squirt; take this nut." I feel his forehead banging against my ass cheeks. He's in deep as I hump his hand; my body is creating inner contractions. I bite down on the pillow and arch my ass higher in the air. This bastard keeps eating, and my juices blow back like a nuclear blast. Any other man would run, but he stays in the fight like the last Spartans facing the Persian army. I left some DNA on his tongue, and I know he's thirsty for more.

He flips me over and throws my legs over my head. I wrap them like a pretzel until I'm in a damn ankle lock. I guess that's why he works out because he drills my pussy with some hard thrusts. Hell yeah, this feels good, and I can take some dick--

especially some dick that I love. I see ripples moving up my stomach as he enters and exits my womb.

"Oh shit, deeper into this pussy, baby. Deeper, deeper. "Yes, that's it," I moan.

"Take this dick like medicine, take it all," Malakai says huffing and puffing.

I pant, "Roll over so I can straddle that dick."

I bounce and grab the head post for extra leverage, because I am about to tame this fucking bull. I go faster, then slowly stop, and twist my ass on his dick real slow, gripping that shit as I turn around because I don't want any of it to slip out; riding backward now, because I am a beast like that. I grab his ankles and bounce my ass up and down on his dick. He begins to slap my ass every time I come down. The pain was sharp, but the pleasure was fucking terrific.

I grip his meat with my walls every time I come down on his shaft. Gently squeeze his nutsack until he lets out a small scream. He loves it when I do that shit. I could feel the nut traveling from his balls. I let his precious jewels go as he coated my pussy with his creamy sauce. I ride and play with my pussy, slapping it, pinching it until the overflow of juices came out. I turn around and tongue kiss my man as he finger fucks my ass hole.

I look at him and say," Don't start nothing you can't finish." He pulls his fingers out of my ass, licks it, and says, "I am Malakai and I spit hot shit."

"A CHURCH MOUSE IS A QUIET PERSON THAT DOESN'T TALK SHIT DURING SEX. STUFF THEIR THROAT WITH DICK AND PUSSY TIL THEY CHOKE ON SPIT."

CHAPTER 19

MALAKAI

We finally exit the interstate and head towards downtown Orlando to Hydro's spoken word spot. Pandora and Asperilla have been talking nonstop, but there's never an unimaginative moment with them around. I need to see what Jaz could do in a club scene, so she and Ayanna are trailing behind me in their brand-new white matte Camaro. That car is so clean that birds refuse to shit on it. The only female that kept one cleaner was this sexy chick in Miami name Casi.

When we get there, the club is live and ready for tonight's erotic takeover. I would be on my gentlemen swag until it's time for me to hit the stage.

I escort the ladies to the front door, and security politely tells us that our VIP booth is ready. There are a lot of Latin ladies in the building, but Asperilla will make sure they all walk under her pussy scent before the night is over. The music is playing, and I must admit that Hydro has come up since the last time I was in this city.

Asperilla interrupts my thoughts. "What's the beef between you and Hydro?"

I gaze into her eyes. "I was wondering when you were going to ask me that. Hydro has been around for a minute, and when I started spoken word, I came here to perform. Well, at least I thought I would perform. I showed up early before any other poets. I even called his cell before I arrived to let him know that I was from out of town and I wanted to spit. I just wanted to make sure my name wasn't overlooked because this poetry game is so cliché and a lot of them only cater to their locals.

"The show started, and I waited patiently for them to call my name. I knew I wouldn't be the first one, but I thought I would go up at least fifth. The names were rolling with all types of talent, and this dude was singing or trying to do a poem after every artist that came up on the stage. He was drunk as fuck, so he lost the first open mic sheet and they gave him another one, but my name wasn't on that one.

"I waited as long as I could, almost three hours, and I still didn't get a chance to bless the mic. A week passed, so I contacted him on the internet. He gave me a whack ass apology, but after that, I told a friend not to visit the spot.

"He heard about it and told me that I give poetry a bad name and to start my own spot if I don't like the way he runs his.

"Well, I did start my own spot, not one, but several and regardless how hot I become as a poet or club owner, I will forever remain humble to the art. Hydro doesn't even remember that it was me at his spot that night."

Before I say another word, the weak bastard climbs on stage to start the show.

"Welcome to another night of Soulful Stimulation! We have the band playing, the bar is serving your favorite drinks, and, of course, we have some of the hottest poets and ladies in the city. Tonight, you are about to experience the most explicit erotic show you have ever seen. We usually battle other erotic crews, but tonight you will see Hydro vs. Malakai for bragging rights," he announces.

As soon as he mentions my name, heads roll over in our direction. I know the ladies will support me regardless, and I can feel all the men in the rooms clutching their dicks. They know that after the first three words, their women will slowly slip from under their arms.

Hydro doesn't waste any time calling me onto the stage and the crowd begins to cheer my name as I walk through the club. I gave Jaz a wink, so she could walk and meet me on the stage. She glides across the floor like a model wearing her black Versace cocktail dress with her fringe stilettos. As we make our way to the stage, Hydro is getting extra cocky, talking about how I can go first and the floor is mine until he comes back up to dethrone me.

He walks up to me and whispers, "Just so you know, your girl promised me some pussy and head for a month if you lose."

I could have easily gotten upset, but I snatch the mic from him and say, "You will never taste or enjoy my leftovers because I'll never lose."

It feels so good to see him speechless for a minute. I grab a chair, the mic stand, and wave my hand for Jaz to join me.

She rocks her hips with each stride, and when she is in my face, she slowly begins to slip out of her dress. Every man in the room begins to say "damn" at the same time, drawing it out with their excitement.

She takes one step out, then the next, and throws the dress into the crowd where men fight to get it while the ladies try to take it.

She stands there with one hand on her hip, wearing nothing but a matching lace bra and thong. After that striptease, all eyes are on us, I strip out of my suit and pull off my pants, revealing my Barocco low rise briefs.

I adjusted the mic stand lower and sit in my seat. Jaz twerks her ass and starts to walk in the perfect cadence. She walks behind me and slides down my chest. Her face is on my nuts while I inhale her scented pussy. I placed the mic close enough to my face that I could spit and not hold it.

I finally speak. "Orlando! Are you ready?"

They start to cheer, and with every scream, Jaz bounces her ass in my face.

"Orlando! Are you fucking ready for Malakai?"

The ladies start their tradition and throw their thongs, boy shorts, and money on the stage. The guys stand up for this one, because they were curious as hell, too. I always put on a good show; never seen nor duplicated because God only made one of me.

I tell Jaz that the time is now. She goes into a slow grind, twirling her hips as I take a slow sip to make every woman wish I was tasting them tonight. Then I let the first verse out, and it's raw and gritty. Jaz sticks her hands in my briefs and starts to play with my dick on stage. I usually don't allow my girls to touch me, but I want to turnout his spot.

I spit with destruction,

I am going to wash my face in your pussy

And gargle your juices.

Blow echoes into your holes

Until my words sees from your knees.

My head you can squeeze until I sneeze cum out

Like a fresh breath of air.

My tongue will sink into your heart

And cause a deep freeze as I lick and slurp.

You want me to get wetter,

Grind your hips upon my nose.

So, I can smell and inhale

As I run these lips through your tail

Like a rummage sale.

I'll flip you over all types of ways, so you ride my face While I
taste and sip your drips.

Moan my name, shout it from your veins,

Rain in my mouth, I have a bottomless pit

That is ready to lickety split you in half.

The power to create an aftermath of destruction.

As your nuts keep busting, juices gushing,

And body thrusting as you squirt down my forehead.

I got you shaking thoughts out of your head.

Slide off my face and slide on my pole.

Grab a fist full of your hair with one hand

And palm your ass with the other.

Pump this dick until your heart jumps.
Twirling my hips in figure eight motions.
Digging in you like a soul food plate.
Grab the back of my head and moan,
"Deeper Malakai, deeper Malakai."
Slap your ass and start to thrust faster and faster.
Bouncing you so hard that I am about
To throw you off this dick,
But you hold on with all your might.
As I shoot this hot lava in you.
Rest your head upon my chest
And just lie there in peace.
I love your wetness, so I take my two fingers,
Dig out our juices and wipe it on my tongue.

When I finish the last line everyone except Hydro stands, even some of his crew is clapping and shit. The dude is so flabbergasted that he waits almost five minutes to come to the stage. I lift Jaz up and tote her back to the VIP section. The crowd is still in awe from the performance. More ladies come over to get my autograph and ask when the next time will be that I perform. Some promise me pussy on the spot; other ladies want me to sign their titties. *I am a Poetic Whore, but I don't just fuck anything anymore;* I laugh to my damn self on that one.

Ayanna came over to the VIP with our extra clothes. She is always welcome to mingle with us, but Asperilla and she would probably fight if they were around each other too long.

"Great show, Malakai," Ayanna says.

"Thank you, Ayanna, and I really appreciate you bringing Jaz and me some extra clothes," I say as I catch my breath. I was dripping sweat, and if I didn't know any better, I'm pretty sure Jaz creamed down my chest for real. That woman is going to turn Florida out real soon.

Ayanna called in the cavalry, and my girls are in full effect to make money tonight. Business comes before pleasure. There goes that chill in my side whenever I mention that word.

I shake it off and continue networking. Hydro finally tries to spit an erotic poem. That's like a virgin trying to take it up the ass before she gives up the pussy. That idiot deserves this torture tonight, and I served him and everyone else up in this place.

I told Ayanna to watch out for the girls, and I promised to keep my phone wide open, just in case something pops off again.

She tells me, "there is a little money in here, but the Magic's players are looking for a few ladies. Since they can't win on the court, they would like to play in our paint."

"You are right on that one," I joke, "enjoy the nightcap. Asperilla, where the hell is Pandora?" I ask.

"She's outside talking to a guy she knows and he will take her home," Asperilla answers.

I chuckle, "Good." *One less mouth to hear in the car,* I think to myself. I have to talk to Jaz first.

"Jaz, I know I told Ayanna to watch you, and she will, but you must always keep your eyes open in this game. These tired-ass fellas will try and test you, and if you're making more money than them, don't fuck with them. Don't discount shit, and you will be fine. I really thank you for performing with me tonight; you are extremely talented on stage. Next time, don't be playing with my dick so much because I could have moisturized your fingers down there."

We chuckled, and I gave her a big hug. I'll see her next week when we fly out to Houston.

She tells me that she is an excellent listener, and she can't wait to head back to her old city. The ladies go their separate way, and Asperilla and I head toward the car. Asperilla tells me that she was proud of me, and even though she doesn't like poetry, she loves me.

"Hell, naw," she says as she stops. "I forgot something."

We run back in, and she goes up on stage and grabs the microphone. What the hell is this retarded woman doing? I am never embarrassed with her, so I just order a drink.

"Hydro," she calls, "if you don't mind, I need you to come to the stage, please."

I guess the fool didn't want to show up, so Asperilla runs off at the mouth. "Orlando, your hometown poet decided to bet me that if

Malakai lost, then I would have to give him head and pussy for a month."

The crowd was shocked. If you thought the poem I did had their attention, this damn woman of mine is fucking their brainwaves.

She screams," Hydro, H20, or whatever your name is, come on up. You said that if you lost, you would give up the door money, and we want our shit."

She looks at me and smiles. "Mr. Hydro also said he would do a poem about wearing ladies panties every time he spits on stage."

Hydro stands up and yells, "That crazy bitch is lying; Malakai, you and your girl need to leave my spot."

Security comes over to me, and some head toward the stage. I know some of you all are thinking that I am worried, but Asperilla is a born hustler while others are trying to learn the game.

She pulls out her phone and replays the conversation Hydro and her had at the mall. The crowd laughs and points fingers at him. His crew knows it's the truth, so they just look the other way.

I keep sipping on my drink, and finally, the punk-ass poet comes on stage and spits his underwear piece.

After he's done, I go over to him. "If you don't mind, kind sir, please give me what is owed to me."

He starts to talk shit, but I keep smiling.

I whisper in his ear, "you should really pay attention to the poets that you diss. I am one of the poets that wasn't worthy to grace your stage back in the day and tonight was payback."

I sing 50 cent's *The Game* chorus.

Hate it or love it, the underdog's on top,
And I'm gonna shine homie until my heart stops.
Go 'head envy me, I'm spoken word MVP,
And I ain't goin' nowhere, so you can get to know me.

CHAPTER 20
MALAKAI

If it weren't for the delays, we would have landed in Houston over two hours ago.

"Welcome to my city," Jaz says as we walk through the airport. She's thrilled to be back home, and she tells Ayanna that she can't wait to go shopping.

I shake my head and laugh, because I know that once they have a taste of pleasure and money, they will forever want more.

"Ayanna, enjoy yourself and don't let Jaz take you anywhere crazy," I insist.

"Did you forget I am from ATL and everyone is crazy there? So, I can assure you that this city, I can handle," she says with a million-dollar smile.

We make it down to baggage claim, and I gather all the luggage.

We exchange hugs, and they head off to rent a nice ride for their adventure. My day is only beginning; I still have to meet Love Divine and learn this piece for Saturday night's show.

I call her, and she answers on the first ring. You have to love a woman that is all about her profession.

"Good afternoon, Ms. Divine, I am staying at St. Regis."

She quickly responds, "You have to stay at a 5-star hotel, such a showoff."

"Meet me at the hotel around four-thirty so we can practice. It's time the world see my poetic sensual side," I mention.

"Can't wait to see it for myself," she chuckles and hangs up.

I'm on my way to pick up my reserved car when my phone starts to ring. I don't recognize the number, so I ignore the bullshit. Then a text comes through.

I know you had something to do with the preacher's death. I will be in touch to collect your body.

This fool must have a death wish to send something like this to my phone. Then leaves 3 smiley faces with the words, *The Punisher*.

I call the number back immediately, but of course, the coward refuses to answer.

Great! Another person wants to play games. There goes my plans to get new connections.

I can't mix new business until I wipe off this old shit. I'll have to fly back and reschedule the meeting. I'll have that number traced when I return to Florida, but I refuse to allow someone to create stress in my life, especially before I touch the mic.

I reached the counter and told her that I have reservation for today. I give her my license, and she starts staring at me. She finally stops when she sees that I've noticed.

"You're Malakai," she says, "all of Facebook is talking about you performing Saturday night at Cafe 4212. I can't believe how humble you are," she says as she hands me the keys.

"Fierce on stage but a lamb in the flesh," I say as I kiss her hand and autograph a CD.

She's delighted and runs around the counter and gives me a big hug and a kiss.

It's moments like these that I love being a poet. I could have easily dipped into that pussy, but sometimes it's not always beneficial to fuck someone that loves your work. Feelings can get in the way and cost me a fan.

"See you Saturday," I say walking to my rental.

Hell yeah! I asked for a Mustang and they upgraded me to a Hummer. The Erotic Gods have shown me favor.

Favor! That's what the church folks be hollering. They get a close parking space to the door at Wal-Mart. Favor! Favor! Let me quit making fun of church folks.

I throw my luggage in the back, start this bad boy up and head straight to the hotel. I found a station playing *Brass Monkey.* I am an old school junkie to the heart. They play classic throwbacks all the way to the hotel.

As I unload my luggage, the valet welcomes me and this hotel is magnificent.

I approach the check-in counter, and the beautiful woman's perfume greeted my nose with a "Good Afternoon, Sir."

"Thanks for allowing me to stay in you all's establishment," I say. "And I would like to know if the room comes with your service."

Before I could finish fucking her mind, I hear someone clearing their throat behind me.

I turn around, and it's Love Divine. "Are you always late?"

"Yeah, unless I'm cumming."

"You are stupid as hell," she says while punching me in the arm.

Damn Cockblocker. Houston, we have a problem.

The woman is smiling and says, "You are on the fifth floor and everything is ready as you requested."

"Thank you and I would like to invite you out to a poetry show Saturday night," I say.

"Do you have any flyers?" She asks. "I can bring some of my girls so we all can maximize the moment with your fine ass," she states.

Love Divine hands her one and says, "The show starts at 8pm."

"Thanks for the compliment and have a lovely day," I say, walking away.

I turn back around, tell Love Divine to follow me and walk like a robot to the elevators.

"You are an idiot; I should record you and post it on WorldStar."

We finally make it to my suite, and she notices the lit fireplace, candles, and the dinner already set in place.

She quickly says, "Damn, you are going all out. I hope you don't think we are fucking."

"Let's enjoy. Let's rehearse these lines. Anyway, you can't say you weren't fed before I put you out," I laugh.

I'm in the zone and ready to spit these lyrics, so I pull out the chair for her to sit down.

I tell her that the truth to being a great poet and businessman is to strategize the future.

"I know your mind is completely blown, but let's sample this great meal and taste each other's words."

I tell her to go ahead and taste the roasted lamb as I pour her a glass of Pinot Noir.

We decide to toast to poetry and friendship, and the wine runs so smoothly down my throat that I pour another glass. She was really in the mood for spitting, because she starts describing how she wants the poem to go Saturday night.

She says, "We will do short verses, one after another; but since you don't always perform collaborations, I will enhance your style with a feminine touch."

"I can't wait for the show. You have all of these rules, so what do I need to wear?" I joke.

"I bought you something to wear because I refuse for you to be naked on my set," she admits.

I laughed and knew from the moment that I met this wonderful goddess, that she was truly a gift given to me by the angels.

Her desire for poetry has me in the mood to get back out into the spoken word scene. I need to hit up as many poetry spots as possible, and maybe I can visit the scene in London. Those ladies and their accents are so sexy.

We finish our meal and go over the piece. I'm in the process of reciting my last line again when I glance at the clock and see that it's after ten.

I'm surprised. We have been at this piece for about five hours. She gathers her things, and I tell her thanks for the lovely evening. She tells me we could have been done hours ago, but we will be performing perfection. I grinned from cheek to cheek because she was right.

I walk her downstairs and wait until her car arrives. When it does, I give her a tight hug and tell her thanks for inviting me here because I needed this break from my everyday life. I watch as the car drives away, and as soon as I start walking back into the hotel, my phone goes off. It better not be that unknown text number again. It's Asperilla. I think I'd rather receive the death threat.

Before I could even say hello, she whispers, "If you wanted to fuck another woman, all you had to do is ask, so I could fuck her too."

"Why the hell are you whispering on the phone? Your ass really needs to see a shrink one day," I say being annoyed.

She laughs, "Hell yeah, you might be right but I called in a favor in Houston; you are not the only one able to make smooth connections. We need to settle our differences and regenerate the business."

I cut her off, "The business has always been fine, and you need to stop doing schemes like the shit you pulled with the pastor."

She says, "Speaking of the Pastor, who else knows that you had him killed off, because I received a wild out text today, and I am pissed as hell."

"I thought it was just me, but it seems someone is trying to exploit us. No need to worry but we have to plan to protect our investments."

She agrees and for the first time in a long time, she ended the phone call with an "I love you." If she had given me enough time, I would have told her that even with her evil ways, I love her, too.

"WHY DOES A GOOD PUSSY ALWAYS HAVE A
PSYCHOTIC WOMAN ATTACHED TO IT?"

CHAPTER 21
ASPERILLA

I would never have thought in a million years that I could love someone, especially a fucking man. I hated all those muthafuckers and, to be honest, the real reason why I am so hard on these escorts is because these prissy bitches working for us have a life of luxury. They have men making love to their ass nightly, earning great money, and living in homes that an average woman couldn't even afford.

I remember when my mama would suck and fuck so we could have food on the table. I still have nightmares about the day I had to go with her to work. She actually had to give a man head with me in the room because the nasty bastard paid extra for me to watch. He humiliated the hell out of my mama that night, and he had the nerve to try and touch me. I was only ten, but I was ready to kill to protect my pussy.

My older cousins taught me how to put a bun up in my hair and hide razors in there for protection. That was the last time he received head because he lost his that night. I sliced his throat so quick that his body drop to the floor while his dick was still hard. My mother and I took the rest of his money and ran out of the room quick as hell.

She told me that our life will never be the same, and we need to head to the US to escape this life. I was served a raw childhood, but I will never let it stop me from making my money.

I like living in this country, but it was my ancestors' land before it was stolen from us.

"Land of the Free" still has some serious issues, but since they can't fix their budget, I'll just keep finding ladies to work the oldest profession.

I pray like hell my past doesn't come back to haunt me. I can't believe I actually told Malakai I love him; maybe it was the text that startled me, and I wanted him to see my true heart, just in case something happens to me.

I can't be soft for love. I know Malakai is about his poetry and the escort business, but I am still on my grind of bloodshed.

Someone sent that text, and I have to do a little more digging before someone decides to take us under once and for all.

We have a lot of envious people out there that want to live in our shoes, but that will never happen as long as my name is Asperilla.

I noticed my phone vibrating, and it's Pandora. She better not be calling to ask about sleeping with Malakai again. I keep telling her silly ass that I am not sharing my dick anymore.

"Pandora, what the hell do you want? I am relaxing for the evening," I say, sounding aggravated.

"Girl, I know you are, but I want to invite you out for a bay cruise next week. A couple of friends are throwing a party on a yacht, and they'll board near Channelside.

"We're sailing," she says, "through Davis Island, the other islands, and the downtown skyline. I already told them that you like to dance, so they promised me that the music would include your favorite songs. They have a gourmet chef that will grill, boil, or whatever you want. The night will be perfect under the stars, and I heard a few football players will be on the yacht as well."

I had to interrupt her, "I guess you will find your future baby daddy?"

"Hell, yeah. I am going panty-less, and when I speak, they will know I can deep throat a football."

"Pandora, your ass is crazy, but you're my girl. You know I'm going, so I can see you act a fool on the yacht. Let me get off this phone and handle my business. I will see you next week, and you already know I will be dressed sexy as hell, because I am a diva."

We hung up, and I pull out a few toys to masturbate myself to sleep. I stole this trick from Malakai since he like to beat his dick to music.

I recommend this tip to every woman that will listen. Get that pussy wet, I mean sloppy wet and then call your man in. Let him dive in face first and balls deep. A dry pussy is like serving a cold dinner and it is the quickest way to find him in another woman's garden. You have to keep the bedroom on fire at all times.

I grab my Happiness and Joy Vibrator and my iPhone, so I could connect my music to the vibrator. I scrolled through my selection and found an old school favorite. Hell, yeah. I am about to tune up this pussy to the one and only Keith Sweat.

I love the bass line drop to *How Deep is your Love.* My hips grind in the sheets instantly as I hear his voice. The vibrator and the mood are perfect.

I pull my hair and do slow jabs into my pussy as the clit stimulator tingles my soul. Damn, this shit feels good as I arch my back to meet every thrust. My toes pop, and I bite my own tongue with excitement.

The session is becoming wetter with each moan; I take my three fingers and open up my asshole, so they won't feel left out of this masturbation tribute. I pull them out and lick them one by one real sensual and long. The slow-motion fucking is incredible as my H&J goes in deeper, but I need to cum like yesterday, so I scroll my hands to the next song. André 3000. Oh, shit. *Hey Ya* comes on, and I pop my pussy all over the bed. I am super soaking these sheets.

I turn up the vibrator to its max speed and stroke to the sound. I sing while I play with my clit like it's a piano. I am a one-woman band that can squirt cum to the audience. I am all into it, and I call out my own name.

"Asperilla, you love me digging in your ass, don't you, bitch? Tell me that you want this nut. Yes, Papi! I love you finger fucking my brains out." You know you are in the zone when you talk to yourself and answer while masturbating.

Juices are running to my asshole, so I act like a DJ and switch the vibrator between my ass and pussy.

I shout, "you think you've got it. Oh, you think you've got it." I am thrusting my hips faster and faster, and I can feel the juices going up my back. I begin to pull the vibrator out and start sucking it like it's Malakai's dick. My fingers are doing the rest as I close my eyes and lick the juices off the clit stimulator.

I am patting and slapping my lips and feeling this nut about to shoot. I am screaming "Alright, alright, alright, alright, alright, alright, alright, alright, alright, alright, alright, alright, alright, alright, alright, alright!

"So, Andre you want to see me on my baddest behavior."

I suck the H&J one last time, open up my pussy, and just push it in real deep and hard. I do it until my eyes roll to the back of my head and my leg shakes. I moan, "yes, yes, fucking yes!" I broke this nut like a woman in labor. I flood my bed and then the song was playing my favorite line.

Ah! Here we go now, shake it, shake it, shake it, shake it, shake it, Shake it, shake it, Shake it like a Polaroid pager! Hey ya!

I take the vibrator out and shake cum all over the bedroom. Some of the juices landed on the wall. Damn, that nut felt so good. I need to get up and clean that shit up before Malakai comes back home, but right now, I lay in my mess and marinate in my thoughts. Well, now when I fall asleep, I don't have to worry about a wet dream, because I am already drenched.

"FUCK MY FACE LIKE YOU PISSED AT IT. I DON'T CARE IF YOU CUM IN MY EYES."

CHAPTER 22

MALAKAI

"Please put your hands together for the Gratifying Goddess known as Love Divine!" After I hear the host announce her, a big smile covers my face. I have been waiting to do this collaboration since I arrived in Houston and the moment has finally arrived. I see the crowd being hypnotized by her looks.

She carries herself quite well; she has the perfect face to wear a low-cut hairstyle. The cashmere tights she's wearing tonight gives her ass a hug in all the right places as her legs flow into her London Trash's thigh high boots. I patiently wait as she steps up to the mic.

"Houston," she moans, "I'm cumming." I'm impressed as she begins to seduce the ears off the crowd.

She tells them to leave all the drama of the world outside because tonight we are about to make love and submerge our thoughts with wet inspirations. She started to slow wind with the syllables she was speaking and I was captivated by her poetic rhythm.

"Tonight, we have a special guest, a nasty, dirty poet. Tonight, he will experience a Love Divine touch," she moans again. "I want to be filled with inspiration from his lyrical penetration."

The crowd is eating up her performance, and I am about to get a hard-on myself, because of the way she's rolling those hips. I am blessed to see her perform as she grinds and speaks soft words.

She finally stops her hips from swaying and whispers to the crowd," Malakai, Malakai, Malakai."

As I walk on stage, I see all the beautiful ladies, and I am thrilled to see the woman from the rental car place. I lean over and gave Love Divine a kiss on the cheek and tell the crowd that I am about to fulfill everything that is Divine. We didn't waste another second. We allow the words to come out of our soul.

My love is
{light} Luminescent at its essence
{light}
Aglow with warm effervescence

My love is {pure}...
Never been mixed with lust or greed
{pure}
Like the medicine or the cure, your body needs

My love is {soft}... as a gentle breeze
{soft}
As a whisper spoken lovingly

My love is {hard}... Like a little kid's head

156

{hard}

Like that deep stroke I bring to bed

My love is {fresh}...

As newly cut grass in summertime

{fresh}

As just picked fruit off the tree

My love is {raw}...

Like being naked, free, and nude

{raw}

Like an outspoken, powerful, impressive dude

My love is {sweet}...

As the sweetest honey made by the sweetest bee. So

{sweet}

You can never drink enough of me.

My love is {sour}...

I can change the expression of your face,

With just a little taste. So

{sour}

That it devours all the other taste buds

When I demonstrate my power.

My love is {ripe}...

As a berry, bursting with juices eager to flow

{ripe}

As a peach; giving under press of fingers on soft flesh

My love is {deep}...

Like that strong voice,

That decision when you can't make a choice

{deep}

With intellect, powerful words to get your brain wet

{deep}

Like the bench of a team, comes in late but leave you

With the ring, dreams, and a

SCREAM... ohhhhh My love is...

Our love.

Our love is {ELECTRIC} sending shockwaves

Up and down my spine,

An electric current flows through my mouth

Whenever I taste your vine

Skin tingling, muscles twitching

Lips become dark, red, and charred,

When I bite on your cord static on my mind riding,

Grinding, and a little sixty-nine is on mine.

Our love is {GRAVITY} pulling me
Into your orbit of being,
I am the Sun and you are the Earth
Get within ten feet of me, and it is ON, here I come

I am the reason why the earth shakes and hums locked
Into your sphere of magnetic pull
I'll charge into your black hole like a stubborn bull.

Our love is {FIRE}
Heat spreads through me like I have a fever
I want to cause friction and combustion
While we are thrusting sweat pours off you,
Drenching me in desire
I want you to sing passion like a choir
As our soul blazes on fire warm and wet to your touch,
Such ecstasy
I want us to cum together, you and me.
Spelling the word L_O_V_E When we come together...
Our {love} Is

As soon as the word "is" left my mouth, she plants a kiss on my lips to seal the deal. I thought I could put on a show, but she has some tricks up her sleeves.

She kisses me with intense passion. I believe she wants me to taste her words, and I was swallowing the metaphors off her tongue. The crowd stands to applaud our performance.

She whispers into my ear, "I knew you have a sensuality inside of that nastiness."

I tell her, "Thanks, you can take credit for this show, because the next one is mine."

She agrees, and she is glowing from the poetry we created, or shall I say the 'Fire we make' like Maxwell and Alicia.

We exit the stage and walk through the back. They had a small open mic after us, so I had a chance to hear some beautiful artists throughout the night.

After the show, I meet some of the performers, sign some autographs, and take pictures with the crowd.

All along, Love Divine is batting her eyes and telling me, "I have to leave in a few."

I say, "I just want to make sure you make it home safely."

She smiles and says, "I'm a big girl, besides I have family here so everything will be fine."

"I am really honored to have shared the stage with you," I say as she hits me in the arm while walking to her car.

"Do you have Alzheimer's? Because you have already said that more than once," she says.

I laugh. "Hell, naw, but if I did, I would always remember Love Divine." I gave her a big hug.

I open the door, she sits down and says, ""Don't worry, Mr. Malakai. I promise to keep your gentlemen side a secret from the street, because I don't want you to lose your status as the Erotic Beast."

I know she wants to cap off the evening with some steamy sex, but I have to focus on these strange ass text messages and I have business to handle in Houston.

She blows her horn and drives down the street.

Tonight is a perfect evening, and it must be my kind of night, because Ayanna is already calling me with new ladies to meet.

"Ayanna, thank you, but we need to abort the mission. I also need you to stick around a little longer. I got a wild text about the preacher, and I guess someone wants to turn the tables on me. I promise to let you walk away with double the money, but I have a strange feeling about this one. I need to start sleeping with one eye open. We have paid our dues from the sheets to the streets, and I'll be damned if any man or woman is going to take a slice of my empire." I confess.

She tells me that she understands and is willing to stay. I also tell her that I need her and Asperilla to get on one accord and resolve whatever issues they are dealing with.

"We have been a family for a long time, and I know I am asking you to swallow your pride, but I promise it will all work out in the end.

"I am flying back to Florida tomorrow but you all can enjoy Houston a little longer."

Ayanna says that she'll relay the message back to Jaz. We hung up, and I immediately dialed Asperilla.

She picked up the phone, and I already knew what she was up to. I tell her that the text message and phone call have me puzzled, as well.

She says, "yeah, I thought you were getting soft, so I was up thinking about who is out there bold enough to try some shit like this."

I tell her to just relax until I come home, and together, we will make sure our business stays top notch. I say, "Asperilla, I forgive you, and I need you on the team. Let's get this money because we can't do this shit forever."

She becomes real quiet, and tells me that she agrees to disagree, then says she is only fucking with me.

She can't wait for me to come home, so we can fuck and figure this shit out.

I tell her wild ass that I love her, and she says she loves me too and will see me real soon. I disconnect the call because there is no way I can tackle this mission alone. I could have easily called Kryptonite to help me, but I dug this hole, so I'll bury the fuckas who think they can shit in my world and wipe it on my doorstep.

CHAPTER 23

MALAKAI

This might not be a bad flight after all. There are some sexy flight attendants working. I should have invested in an escort business for the skies; that would have given a whole new name to the cockpit. I laugh at my own damn self on that one.

Ayanna told me that she would stay a few more days with Jaz to make sure she stays out of trouble since she is bringing her into the family. I told her that would be fine plus I needed to clear my head for the problem that lies ahead.

Before I could bleed another thought out, the flight attendant reaches across my seat saying I need to buckle up. I was like whatever, I know she wants to touch my dick. I've had my seatbelt on since I sat down.

I must be a magnet for pleasure because I am always attracting women that want it. Any other time, I would have been in the bathroom, fucking her from behind, eating that pussy on that little ass sink, while she gives me head as I sit on the toilet.

I tell her thanks, and it's an honor to fly where the women want to make sure that my dick and I land safely. She smiles and keeps on twisting that ass down the aisle.

Sometimes I sit back and wonder why the pleasure of pussy always causes the downfall of a man. As a poet, I always stay in the realm of creativity. One day, I will spit a piece about how Adam lost his kingdom over pussy. When Eve was tempted, Adam's punk ass should have protected his queen. If he hadn't been pussy whipped, he could have easily asked God to send him another woman. I mean, a life of luxury for another rib. I would have given God a whole slab so I could enjoy my garden. Yet he stayed with her and decided to sin as well. So, does that make the devil the first pimp in the world? He laid down the smoothest lines on Eve and had her turning tricks in the garden. That's why a Poet with a treacherous mouthpiece can melt the panties off a woman and have her mentally finger fucking herself while listening.

Enough of that wild thinking for now. I can hear the captain on the intercom telling the flight attendants to prepare for take-off. I always choose a window seat, so I can watch the beautiful skies of heaven.

I thought about Love Divine and how she told me that she couldn't wait to see me in Tampa again. She is truly an amazing and gifted angel with the power to soothe any savage beast. I will ask her to create an album with me to produce magic.

We ascend to the right altitude and are free to walk around the cabin, but since I have so much room in First Class, I'll stretch out and log onto my computer. Moments like this, I love to read some poetry to help me strategize something wicked and unheard of for my foes.

I was a whore before the escort business, but not because I fucked a lot. I always whore through other poet's work which is something that will never end, thanks to Facebook.

I scroll through my newsfeed and this New Orleans chick named Ms. Creoleness captures my attention.

She has a poem with a line in it saying, *I want you to fuck me like a vulture, so I can cum like a swan. Transform this pussy!*

That Creole dread headed bitch's pussy must be connected to her mouth, because she is always cumming, coming with some serious poetry. She is sexy with a cute-ass smile. I'll make sure to contact her real soon about doing a show. I see why she totes wet wipes in her purse, dripping pear juices all down the street and shit. I usually read more than one artist, but after that piece, I'm going to log off this computer, close my eyes, and pray that we are back in Tampa when I wake up.

I'm only half asleep when I feel someone tugging on my pants. The seatbelt is being loosened and pulled apart. I slowly open my eyes and see the flight attendant lifting out my dick.

I could say something, but I am going to allow her to Einstein me. I go with the game and let her suck my dick. I guess there will be a snake on the plane this afternoon.

She never looks up, head just bobbing up and down in slow motion. She is a deep throater, no choker as she continues to serve me.

She licks the tip of my head like ice cream and spits drool all down the side of my dick.

I grabbed a fist full of her hair and stroked her mouth with precision. As she moans and sucks, I freestyle some wild and crazy poetry.

Just in case there is an open space in your mouth.

This dick will deploy to your tonsils compartment.

To secure this nut I am about to shoot.

I need you to close your mouth

And breathe through your nose

As I bring your face close to my abs.

Even if you start to gag

Because of the increase tempo,

Keep in mind that this nut is coming.

Please make sure to catch this nut.

And swallow before assisting others.

I made that up after listening to the oxygen mask safety briefing.

I am laughing to myself because who thinks of crazy shit like that. I want to hurry up and flood her mouth, so I place both hands around her head and keep accelerating this dick into her cockpit. *Fuck, yeah; she is a First-Class Flight Attendant.*

I reach down and play with her titties; she slurps louder and harder.

I am not sure who is watching this show, but at this moment, fuck them too. This white chick must want some chocolate; her head moving like a slinky, and I can't wait to impregnate her throat.

I can feel the nut traveling from my balls, and at this angle, it feels like it's heading to my stomach before it makes a U-turn.

"Bitch," I moan, "Taste me. I am about to cum so be ready to swallow."

Her head game is good but she can't catch it all. She swallows a little but spits the rest back up on my dick and pants.

She gets off her knees and walks away. I feel the juices leaking through my pants.

I woke up and the stewardess was never there. I was like *hell naw!* I know I didn't just dream this shit. I look down at my pants and can't believe I had a wet dream. I know some fellas would be like, "what the hell," but a nut is a nut. I'll take it any way it breaks out. Good thing I'm wearing jeans because that will help conceal it.

I can really use those wet wipes Ms. Creoleness has all the time.

I go to the claustrophobic bathroom and clean my dick. I look into the mirror and smile. I wash my hands and clean cum juice off my underwear. I wonder if I really arched my back in my sleep. Well, someone will be sure to write a story about that one.

I hear the captain asking everyone to return to their seats and prepare for landing. I exit the bathroom, take my seat, and buckle up.

It must have been twenty minutes or less, because the wheels are touching down in Tampa.

The flight attendant flashes a big-ass smile while she thanks me for flying with Delta.

I tell her thank you while grabbing my carry on and exiting the plane. Asperilla and I will have an intense few weeks but nonetheless, I'm delighted to be home.

I called Cherry to ask how she was feeling. It has been almost a month, and she has fully healed; she still wants that man dead and I owe her that wish.

She says, "Everything is fine, except for the crazy shit Asperilla has us participating in."

I respond, "There is no need to explain anything, and Asperilla will not do anything to you or any other woman."

She tells me, "I haven't saved any money like the rest of the ladies, so please don't leave the business until I can afford to be on my own."

I give her my word, because the Houston connection, or any other city I choose, has been placed on hold until I find out who's fucking with me. I tell her that Ayanna will be back this week, and she will help her invest into a new dream while satisfying the clients' reality.

She tells me thanks and promises that she won't let me down again.

I tell her that I will talk to her later, and to be careful. We end the phone conversation as I approach the baggage claim, retrieve my luggage, and walk to the parking deck. I can see my rims shining on my Enzo from here, and I'm ready to speed down the interstate. I love this car. It reminds me of the Bat mobile; I guess I'm the poetic Bruce Wayne.

I drop my computer bag in the seat and call Asperilla," I will be home in less than an hour."

Asperilla says, "I miss you, Papi, and I cooked."

I think I am going to throw up because she never cooks, with good reason.

She says, "I was taught at an early age to do a lot of things; besides, I am turning over a new leaf."

I tell her, "I appreciate you in my life, and I will see you shortly."

Well, since she is trying to change, maybe I'll keep this dick on paper and only wet up the ladies ears; time will tell.

"LOOK IN YOUR EYES AS OUR TONGUES RAGE A FIGHT FOR SUBMISSION. I'M GOING TO MAKE YOU LOVE ME BEFORE YOU CUM FOR ME."

CHAPTER 24

ASPERILLA

Tonight, I'm meeting up with Pandora to attend a party on the yacht. I need a break because I have been racking my mind senseless trying to figure out these crazy messages and notes; they are really getting personal.

I went to the salon to get my hair done, and when I came outside, there was a note stuck to my windshield wiper. I read that bullshit and the steam rose off my skin. The note said, *Tick, Tock. How long it will be before you are living in a cell block? Yours truly, the Punisher.*

I threw that shit in the trash. What kind of idiot tries to emulate an action hero? Well, they will find justice real soon, and it won't be a pretty picture.

I have to stop thinking of that garbage, so I can finish getting dressed. I don't want to be late since Pandora is picking me up for a change. I am always fussing at her for making me wait, so I refuse to allow her the opportunity to do the same to me.

Malakai is downstairs in the den working on a plan to find the attacker and the source of the Punisher, so I know his ass is staying home. Pandora really wants to have a night out. We haven't had one since the trip to Orlando. Hell, we haven't even fucked each other since the encounter with Malakai and we won't be fucking tonight. I believe I have sucked and ridden my last piece of plastic. I know that shit is adventurous, but I need meat between me and my teeth.

I slip on my stilettos and head downstairs to tell Malakai that I'm going out for the evening. I open the door and he is standing there, shirtless and looking over some paperwork. That man does have a wonderful ass, and that's why I stay firm and tone. I never want to walk around with a man whose butt is bigger than mine.

I shout his name, "Malakai?"

He turns around with a charming smile, "Yes, baby?"

I say, "I'm going to a yacht party to get a break from the madness."

He looks at me, "What? You're not staying out 'til sunrise?"

I give him my serious face saying, "Not tonight. I'm learning how to cater to my man."

He gives me a hug and whispers in my ear, "Be careful and I love you. Asperilla, after this drama, I think we should have a baby."

I quickly lie, "hell to the naw! I ain't about to mess up my sexy-ass body"; but deep down, I wouldn't mind having at least two.

He says smiling, "One day, I will fill you up with so much cum, that you will spit out more babies than I can spit rhymes."

I laugh at his nonsense for a minute, turn around and points toward my right ass cheek saying, "You can spit on this if you like, but you're not doing shit to me unless I agree."

He waves his hand like, whatever. "Keep your eyes open and have a wonderful evening."

I go in closer to his face and give him one of the most intense kisses we have ever shared. It takes him by surprise. I should cancel with Pandora tonight, but the doorbell was ringing.

"You better leave before I fuck you on this desk," he yells.

"Yeah, you are right but don't wait up. Keep that dick up so it can sleepwalk in this pussy," I say.

"Girl, get your nasty ass out of here," he jokes.

I say," I'll leave for now, but best believe you are going to choke on this chocha. I am going to flush your face with so much juice, you're going to think it's a running toilet. Now, as y'all poets say, end piece." I exit stage left, leaving the grand lyricist speechless.

Pandora is standing at the door when I open it. She's wearing her 'fuck me in every hole' dress. Before she could say one word, I say, "Bitch I'm ready. Let's go!"

She gives me a crazy look, I tell her that the night is young, and I am ready to salsa my ass off on the boat.

We leave in her convertible Jag, and I love the breeze as we travel to Channelside.

She is so turnt up; dancing and driving crazy as hell. I give her a look like she was stupid and to act her damn age. If we crash, I am going to kick her ass from heaven to hell. She calls me a party pooper and tells me to relax and just enjoy our lovely evening together.

We arrived safely at Channelside, and I stepped out the car into the beautiful atmosphere. I know a lot of people love Miami, but I can do so many things in Tampa and still visit South Beach.

The gentlemen are looking sexy, and it seems they were getting finer and finer as we approach the gate. I tell Pandora that we don't have to get on the boat; the fellas are out tonight.

She promises the boat will have more men than I can imagine and ten times sexier than the ones out here.

I find that hard to imagine, but I will go along with her story for now.

Pandora hands the guy our tickets, and they have a black brother dressed up as a sailor lead us to the top deck. I have to admit, he is handsome. So, she gets a few points for tonight. He begins to give us a tour of the vast yacht.

I can say so far so good, but its quiet on the boat, and all the ladies are on one side. The only man that I see was the one that escorted us here. This bitch better not had brought me to a lesbian party without telling me. I look her in her eyes and say, "you know I am going to kick your ass when we get off this boat, right?"

She laughs and tells me, "just relax, because the night is young, remember? Your reward will come on a silver platter."

Out of nowhere, the DJ starts playing "Shake" by Ying Yang and Pitbull; fifteen male strippers come up the stairs, dancing their asses off. They're throwing dicks and the ladies go into a frenzy making it rain all over the place.

One of them is so fine, he reminds me of a younger version of the Rock, the wrestler with those tribal tattoos all over his chest. He has a long-ass tongue, licking his own nose and grinding the floor. He is one of the best dancers out of the men, and he has my attention.

I place a Ben in his pocket while saying," I love the way you move."

He says, "Gracias, Mamacita," and slowly humps my leg up.

Any other time, I would have done my split and danced on his dick, but I need to get myself a drink.

They keep dancing for a few more minutes, and the DJ does his famous scratch and everything comes to a halt. Another handsome man walks and speak on the mic, "Welcome to *Passionate Pearls*, where you can sail into your wildest fantasies."

I think it's a cool name for a ship. There's no telling what I would have called it; probably *Cunnilingus Crusades*, or something.

He tells us, "We won't be getting too wild; we don't want to end up in jail, but everyone will have the time of their lives."

He claps his hands and fifty well-dressed gentlemen come from the lower deck. Finally, the party is getting started, because there is entirely too much estrogen floating on this boat.

I walk to the bar for a simple Bacardi Cocktail and I see Pandora doing what she does best. She is always looking for the next man to scam on in life, so she can quit working and just party.

I would have put her on my team years ago, but she's not street smart.

She smiles. "Asperilla, I would like for you meet Jerrod, he just moved here from Jacksonville."

I don't want to seem rude, so I politely extend my hand, "It's nice to meet you."

He's a nice-looking man, but my street sense is telling me not to trust him.

Pandora says, "I am going to the bar to get some drinks. We can vibe and party with each other."

I tell her, "That's fine." as we keep talking about his new career in Tampa.

He tells me," Jacksonville was okay, but I heard this city can change a man's life."

I'm looking right in his eyes as he's feeding me this bullshit. His whole swag is fake, just like that stanky-ass cologne.

"So, what made you come to the yacht party tonight?" I ask.

"I was invited out," he replies.

Before he can finish, I interrupt him. "Where are they?"

"What "they" are you talking about?" He snaps.

"Your friends, only a man of great stature would come alone, and I don't see that in you."

"Is this how you get to know a new friend?" he smiles.

"No, this is how I get to know my enemies and I don't trust you. When you point out your friends that you came with or invited you, then I will be more open to talk."

I do my signature Dorothy's heel clicks and say, "there is no place like home," and walk away. I headed to the bar and find Pandora.

I tell her, "stay the hell away from him; there is something that I don't like about him."

"He is really nice, and I would like to get to know him. Damn, I am not trying to marry the nigga. I just want to enjoy the evening," she explains.

I walk away saying, "fine! Enjoy the loser; the view will entertain me," as I snatch my drink from her hand.

I request *There's Some Hoes in this House* by A-Dub. The song plays, I seductively grind my hips making Pandora's old stripper moves look like a two-step.

An Italian man dances with me, and I am so pissed at Pandora for introducing me to Jerrod's punk ass, that I don't even care at this moment.

After the song finishes, I thank my friend with a kiss on the forehead and walk away. I order five shots of Screaming Orgasm, because I need a fucking release. I relish the rest of the night alone while Pandora talks to that cunt mouth bitch.

The DJ spins all the throwbacks with a touch of new school, and I vibe within my own mind. A few gentlemen came up, ask my name and ask if I would I like to dance, but I decline. I just want this night to end. The worst blessing a dude can receive is coming on to a woman after she tells him in a nice way that she'd rather be left alone. I am so glad these fellas didn't cross that line because it would have been an ugly moment.

I dance to the next song in my seat when I feel my head spinning. I knew it wasn't from the shots.

"Aww, fuck nah, Dammit!" I mumble.

Someone drugged my drink and my vision is getting blurry. I hit the panic code on my phone to reach Malakai.

I walk towards Pandora, but that bitch is nowhere in sight, or I just can't make her out from the rest of the people. I stumble while praying my ass don't fall off and drown in the river. I sit down, and some men try to help me, but all their voices sound the same except for one.

I'll remember it for the rest of my life.

"Bitch, you belong to me now. So, let's see how much power I have in my stature now."

CHAPTER 25

MALAKAI

It has been an hour since Asperilla left and I am still backtracking through these photos and papers. I need a break my damn self before I go insane. My club is having a Reggae night, so I know that's out the question but I grab my laptop and do what I am famous for, *whoring*.

My search leads me to Saint Pete, a spot called *Visionary*, and there's a show tonight. Sometimes, it's a blessing to listen to other poets while they share their dreams and passions.

The show starts in an hour, which will give me enough time to shower, dress, and head out.

I know the love of poetry is in the air, and I can taste her essence. This will allow me to ease my mind about these dumb ass text messages and then I can go back to the drawing board.

I get dressed, look in the mirror, grab my car keys, set the alarm, and I'm off to the show.

I'm speeding down the highway and think about that freaky ass officer. Just because I am turning over a new leaf doesn't mean I will stop thinking of my fuck rides.

I guess I am a whore in rehab, because I will fuck again, but I will do my best to fuck the paper. That's my new thing, fuck the paper and cum in their ears.

I have at least fifteen more minutes before I reach Saint Pete, and even though I have celebrity's status, I like to be early. I consider myself no different from any other poet.

I drive down I-275, reach the Baywalk, and find a place to park. I can walk five minutes to the spot. I hear Neo Soul coming out the door as I stand in the line. They're playing my favorite song *Closer*; Goapele is one sexy-ass, mind-blowing artist.

I make it to the door, pay five dollars, and the woman says with an emotional hug, "Welcome to Visionary, where poetry lives in 3D."

I tell her, "thank you," as I head to my seat. I notice a few other poets here so exchanging poetic love is natural for me.

I love a place that starts on time, and the host hits the stage a minute before and performs his piece. The snaps are in full effect tonight, and I feel like I am in a realm where only goddesses and kings roam.

He comes back to the mic and says the next performer on the list is none other than the enchanting and everlasting beauty, Ms. Love Divine.

I stand on my feet, knowing I'm about to have my ears stimulated by one of the sexiest poets on the planet. My heart skips a beat because I had no idea that she would be here. She motions to the band, and they play the smoothest sound known to man. She spreads her vocals and the whole room sways like an ocean wave as her artistic rhythm.

She finishes her piece and goes over to her friends, who are just as gorgeous as she is.

I walk over and ask, "Is this seat taken?"

"Not for the man whose wordplay produces orgasms," she smiles and speaks.

I chuckle and say, "Whatever," and take a seat.

After the last poet, the host comes back and thanks everyone for coming. He asked me to perform earlier but I wanted to listen to the other artists. I bought a few CDs, and exchanged phone numbers so I can book them as features at *Poetic Heaven* in the future.

Love Divine's friends approach us about heading to the club but she has ignored them for most of the night. They laugh and say it's okay, you can enjoy the night with Malakai.

Love Divine looks at me and says, "You know you made me miss my damn ride home."

I tell her, "I promise to get you home safely." She smiles and says, "Thanks for the protection."

We walked downtown to admire the beautiful city. I tell her that her voice is incredible, and I would like to do an album with her.

She tells me, "I would be honored as long as you keep the vulgarity down."

I say, "I am able to spit some clean, sensual pieces."

She laughs, "Barely."

I respond, "You're right."

We walk around town for another hour and I am stress free. I guess I spoke too soon since the panic code came through my phone.

I ask, "Is it okay to call your friends to take you home?"

Surprisingly she asks, "Is everything okay? You are starting to scare me."

I reply," Something urgent has come up, and I don't want you involved."

She answers, "Ok, let me call them now."

"Malakai, they are already in Tampa," she explains as she hangs up.

"Fuck it. I will drop you off, let's go," I say as we run to the car.

I tell her to buckle up and I promise not to scare her too much. I know I love the hell out of Asperilla because I have never moved this fast.

I pull out with the tires screeching and don't give a damn. I am so glad that I had her phone synced with a tracking device. I drive like a fucking bullet out of a gun, and Love Divine doesn't flinch one time.

We got to the location without wrecking shit, and I tracked her phone to the marina at the Westshore Yacht Club. This place is dark and creepy. I feel this is an ugly set up, but I have no other options.

"Love Divine, stay inside the car until I get back," I ordered.

"No problem. Just be careful," she requests.

"I promise to explain everything tomorrow but for right now, just don't ask," I say as I take my 9mm out of the glove compartment.

I call Ayanna while approaching the yacht, "Asperilla is in trouble. I'm at the Westshore Yacht Club and if you don't hear from me in ten minutes, call the police. You know where everything is just in case something goes wrong."

"Yes, I know. I will be waiting for you to call me back," she speaks calmly then hangs up.

I go on-board, start my search but I am watching my back with every step.

I hear steps behind me; I move fast enough to catch him off guard as soon as he turns the corner. I stand behind the door and this idiot walks right past me. I knock him on the back of the head with the pistol and his gun flies out of his hand.

He falls to the ground and I bash his face a few times screaming, "Where the fuck is Asperilla?"

I stand up and kick him in the ribs for not answering my question.

I cock my pistol and ask him again, "Where the fuck is Asperilla? And if you say the wrong thing, I promise you won't make it off this boat."

"Oh, I will be alive but you won't," he chuckles. He falls as I punch him in his face for talking shit.

"Get up, you stupid bitch! I am not done with you yet," I yell. Dragging him off the boat, I notice another guy holding Love Divine at gunpoint.

JERROD

"Come on down, Mr. Malakai, the price is right. I have this bad bitch for sale," he says as he starts licking her face.

"Get your hands off me!" Love Divine screams.

"Just like a pussy ass nigga, using a woman for bait. If anything happens to her, I promise your heart will be pulled out and fed to the fishes," Malakai points and yells.

"You ain't gonna to do shit but toss that pistol in the water and let my partner go," I smile.

"Divine, I am truly sorry for getting you into this," he says while throwing his gun.

Jermaine turns around and punch Malakai in the face. "Who's the bitch now?" Jermaine shouts.

"Malakai!" She yells.

"Shut up, hoe, before I slice your fucking throat," I snap.

"You really need to let her go. Who the fuck are you anyway?" he says while spitting out blood.

"I'm the one that beat the shit outta your hoe at the hotel. Here! You can have your bitch's phone back since she's at the county jail," I say while tossing the phone. "By the way, nice tracking device. Just so you know, my name is Jerrod," I say sarcastically.

"Divine, I promise everything will be ok. Jerrod just let her go," he pleads.

"Jermaine, hold my pistol and if that fuck nigga even blinks his eyes, shoot him," I demand.

"Bout time, that fucker pushed me down the stairs and I can't wait to squeeze a round off," Jermaine says.

"You see, Malakai, we aren't that different. You sell pussy, I take pussy; you make money, I take money. We both love bitches; you just made a mistake by bringing one here. I should rape this hoe right here. With you out of the picture, your business is wide open. I'll have my choice of any woman I want," I brag.

"Fuck you, Jerrod!" he yells.

"You are still talking shit. You are in no position to say nothing," I smile. I look over at the woman by my side. "You are such a pretty woman and I hate to split you open," I say pulling out my knife.

"Malakai, save yourself! Please don't worry about me," she yells.

"Go ahead bitch and scream he can't save you," I say. whispering in her ear.

"I haven't got all night for this bullshit. Malakai, since you like to slice things off; this should bring back memories," I say, slicing her throat.

"Damn! Jerrod, you are ruthless!" Jermaine shouts.

"You ain't seen nothing yet," I laugh as her body falls to the ground. "One down, one more to go," I say while putting my knife back.

"Jerrod, you better kill me because I promise you will pay for this. I don't give a damn how long it takes I am going to bury you and your whole fucking family," Malakai says.

"Talk is cheap. Jermaine shoot this nigga!" Jerrod says.

Jermaine unloads the clip into Malakai as I watch the bullets hit his legs, arms, and chest. His ass falls to the ground.

"Make sure you finish his ass off," I yell.

Jermaine walks over and shouts, "Bitch, I told you that you wouldn't make it out of here alive," firing another shot and kicking his ass in the water.

"What the fuck? Why you kick his ass in the water? We need to make sure his ass is dead," I scream at Jermaine.

"Look, Jerrod, he is fucking dead; I shot his ass 6 times. Let's get the fuck out of here before the police come; I know someone heard gunshots," he insists.

You talk a lot of shit for a nigga that almost had his face kissed by a bullet; remember I saved your punk ass tonight. I don't even see his body floating back up. You better hope he's dead."

"Whatever, nigga. Let's go. I will never send a rookie to do a man's job again."

"What the fuck you mean by that?" Jermaine asks.

I pulled out my gun and fired two shots in his head. "Bitch! That's how you make sure someone is dead."

CHAPTER 26

ASPERILLA

I am a little drowsy but opening my eyes, the smell alone only means one thing. I am at a fucking police station.

"Rise and shine, sleepy head. You have been out for a minute. We have been looking for you. So, is the word on the streets true? Are you the infamous Asperilla Valdez; the woman who masterminded the death of the beloved Pastor?" the detective spoke.

"Word on the street is how the Pastor bought pussy on Saturday, and then spit cum lies on Sunday. Riddle me that Batman, because I see nothing beloved about a man that plays with God peoples and their money," I say.

"You have a smart mouth but all that will change when we place your pretty ass in jail. We'll see how long you can last with real criminals as roommates," he says.

"Sir, what is your name again? And how the hell did I get here when I was on a yacht a couple of hours ago?" I ask.

"I am Detective Stevens and I welcome you to the Hillsborough County Sheriff's Office, where you will be residing until you produce some answers. I see you coming in here with your pedicured nails, long hair, and sweet voice but you are a snake and going to down for the murder of Pastor Johnson. To answer your question, we received a tip about a drunken woman on a yacht claiming that she murdered a local Pastor," he answers.

"Excuse me, Detective, or shall I say Dick-tective. All you have is some bullshit about what I supposedly have said at a party. I am innocent but continue on threatening me with a little jail time because where I am from, we hold beauty pageants in prisons. I won a few so go ahead and send me somewhere to enhance my sexiness," I say proudly.

I could tell that he is not used to a woman talking to him like that but I continue on stirring shit. "Let me ask you another question. Do you talk to your wife like this when ya'll are fucking, all macho and shit? If not, you should because while you are all in my face, I can guarantee you that another man is beating her pussy down in your sheets right now. If you don't believe me, call your house, and put the conversation on speakerphone because you are a genuine fuck boy."

"What did you just call me, bitch?" he yells.

"A fuck boy, built like a man but fucks like a little boy. Now you know the real reason why she is guzzling someone else kids down her throat as we speak. So, when you kiss her, you will always taste a piece of someone else's child support. Now interrogate that, Dick-tective," I laugh in his face.

"Bitch, if we weren't in this office, I would teach your ass a fucking lesson about respecting real authority," he says, gritting his teeth and grabbing my hair.

"Go ahead, Papi. I love being punished for being naughty. Let me see your veins pop," I laugh as he raises his hand to slap me, then the door opens.

"Stevens, put your damn hands down and let the woman go! I'll take it from here. You need to go outside and cool down," the voice says.

He releases my hair, looks at me, and says, "you are one lucky bitch for now."

He pounds his fist on the desk and walks away. The other detective walks over and pulls up a seat.

He calmly says, "Good Morning, I am Detective Holiday."

I say, "Good Morning," and sing, "It's a beautiful day in the neighborhood, a beautiful day in the neighborhood. Would you be mine? Could you be mine?"

He interrupts me, "How cute. The monster can sing too. Listen, I'm not here to bullshit you; I just want to know the truth about the Pastor. Why you were at his church a couple of months ago and are you responsible for his death? I have church members that can verify you were with an unknown gentleman and you two disrupted their morning service."

At that particular moment I knew I was set up, but the facts weren't in place so there was no need to worry.

I have to buy some time, so I respond, "I need to call my lawyer before answering anymore questions."

"Your ass should call Johnny Cochran to help you from the grave," he says while walking out.

I need a moment to rethink. *Where the hell is Malakai and what is taking his ass so long to find me?* I am replaying all these thoughts in my mind. If there had been a witness at the church that could have placed me there, then they would have arrested me and Malakai last month. I will wait this one out; I know it is someone close to us that is trying to corrupt our business and put me away.

It is really odd that I am here and haven't heard a word from Pandora. I knew that it was Jerrod that whispered into my ear before I passed out. I wonder if he kidnapped her and left her for dead somewhere. The only person I can call is Ayanna but her face doesn't need to be seen anywhere near a police station. I'm going to dig out every conversation I have had with enemies and acquaintances and figure out who is playing the role of Judas.

When I see Malakai, I am going to slap his face sideways for leaving me in here. As for Pandora, this is all her fault for inviting me to that damn party. I know Jerrod is not executing this plan alone; he is too simple-minded to pull off something of this magnitude. His ass couldn't even tie his shoe without getting his finger caught in the loop.

Hell, I need to make a phone call. I tapped the door for the officer to come in. These fuckas should have handcuffed me because I am really dangerous to their health.

I told the officer that was watching the door that I needed to place a phone call. The best thing about Malakai and this underground fuck business is that he is always on some James Bond type shit. I am good at scheming but Malakai keeps his head into the future. He always thinks of ways to cover up all the "what ifs". This morning, I am delighted that I remembered how to use the phone to send messages without saying a word.

I dial Ayanna's phone and punch a numerical tune so she would know that I was in jail and I haven't heard from Malakai. After the last number was dial, the phone line went silent. I know the detective thinks I called my lawyer and I am sweating bullets but Asperilla Valdez only sweat while getting her back broke during a hard fuck.

Speaking of the detective, the idiot that pull my hair came up to me with another crazy look on his face.

"My boss told me that I have to be real nice to you from now on. Mark my words, one day I'm going to catch you outside and I will fuck up that pretty little face of yours," he chuckles.

"I'll make sure your wish comes true if you are man enough to tango with this Mamacita," I say swaying my hips.

He grabs my arm and tells me, "Your smart ass can dance to this holding cell."

We walked down the hall and I could see everyone staring because they knew beauty has arrived.

We finally reached the holding cell and he threw me on the ground.

"There you go, be a good puppy," he says trying to embarrass me.

So, to keep him entertained, I bark and whine. He slams the door but I didn't give a damn. This cell isn't bad at all and exactly what I need to get my thoughts together.

I can visualize everyone on the yacht including the faces of each stripper. I can even smell Jerrod's cologne that gave me a headache, which probably was the drug that caused me to blackout. Let me stop joking before I actually spend more time in prison then I should. The host was kind of funny acting but I knew he didn't have a reason to harm me.

I mumble to myself, "Think Asperilla, fucking think. If someone wanted your empire and wanted to take you down, who would it be?" Damn, there was so much action on the top deck last night that it is causing my brain to overload. I won't give up until I can piece this puzzle together.

I can see drinks, Malakai, Jerrod, Pandora, Pastor Johnson, and a murdering plot. I know I am missing something out of this equation or should I say someone.

I twist the end of my hair and the more I pull, the deeper my mind went back in time. I really don't give a fuck if I have to pull every damn strand out of my fucking head. I need to know who wants to see me buried behind these walls.

Right now, I refuse to trust anyone because they all might be plotting. Somewhere between those four names lies the answer to my question. I know Jerrod hates me with a passion, Pandora wants to fuck Malakai so she has been pissed since I refuse to share him.

Malakai, I love you with all my heart but you are a dead muthafucker if you are plotting against me.

Fuck, these four walls are getting the best of me. I have to shake this feeling off real quick. He wouldn't do anything like that;

we have been through some storms but we do have an honor code. He did say that he is tired of my shit.

I felt my first tear run down my face and hit the floor. I tap the tip of my fingernail in the small puddle. I know what Jesus endured a little bit to be beaten and lied on; these bastards are trying to convict me of a crime I didn't commit. I won't rise like him on the third day but I will claw their eyes out.

I tap my fingernail faster, thinking about who would benefit more with me and Malakai out of the picture. A sinister smile lit up my whole face. *Malakai, I am so sorry that I thought you would ever betray me. I should have known better but I'll figure out who is behind the notes, texts and the phone calls.*

I should have thought of that bitch from the beginning; damn, I slipped on my black widow instinct. They say when you fall in love, you become blind sometimes. I didn't see this one coming at all and that only means one thing; someone on our team is helping her out too. I'll sit in jail and plot on how to kill that bitch. This is far from being over. As Tupac would say, "revenge is the sweetest joy next to gettin' pussy."

"HAVE YOU EVER HAD YOUR DICK SUCKED
WHILE SHE FINGER-FUCK YOUR BUTT. OH
FUCK!"

CHAPTER 27
JERROD

I enter the house to see the ladies on the couch kissing each other. I guess they are tongue stroking their victory down each other throat. They didn't even look up once to see me standing in the room.

"Excuse me, Pussy Bandits. Why are you two in here having the time of your life? I want my damn money and I mean all of it. I did all the work, from drugging Asperilla to killing Malakai. I even had to take an innocent woman's life.

"Now back to business, this is my routing and account numbers; I am about to leave for a while. This city is about to be shaken up by the police and I don't want to be anywhere around when they come," I order.

Serenity said, "Relax, baby. I promise you will have everything by tomorrow. No need to worry about the police, they work for me now. Now since you love business so much, are you sure that Malakai is dead? Because he is the only one that can stop Asperilla from going to jail forever.

"I want her to suffer behind bars for a while; next month we will pay her a visit. I can't wait to see the look on her face when we show up. I know she will shit a brick inside of her pants when she looks into my eyes."

"Yeah, he is dead and the only poetry he will be performing is the one in hell. He can write a poem down there about being Satan's Bitch," I say.

"You are so hateful, Jerrod. Allow us to make you feel better. You were always envious of your friend's adventures so lie down and we will make you feel like a King," Pandora says.

Pandora unzips my pants and Serenity kisses my earlobe. My dick is seconds away from getting the attention and desires it's been yearning.

Serenity slowly penetrates my ear canal and the wetness runs into my brain as Pandora pulls my belt to the side with her teeth. I closed and reopened my eyes to make sure this wasn't a dream. I lift my butt up so Pandora can slide my pants to my ankles. I kick my shoes off and pull my boxers down so they could see my King Kong ready to swing throughout their deepest jungle.

Serenity nibbles on my neck and takes slow bites from my right ear to my left ear. She stops in front of my mouth and unleashes her tongue down my throat.

Pandora plays with my dick, stroking it nice and slow, and massaging the tip with her saliva. I enjoy the moist breeze from her mouth as she expands her suction cup to force my dick in. She licks my balls and slightly pulls on them with her teeth.

Serenity stands up, undresses and her body is incredible; she has the looks of Angela Bassett.

She swaps positions with Pandora as she takes her clothes off and returns to her duty.

I pull my shirt off, toss it to the side as the ladies lick each other tongues and take turns sucking on my dick. They really know how to make a man weak in the knees.

I see the power and love as they finger each other's pussy. They create an idyllic movement, with one sucking my dick while the other finger fucks.

I watch them share sensual kisses as they provide the best hand job known to man. I am under their command and every moan they make stiffens my dick.

I grab Serenity's hand and tell her to fuck my face and don't stop until I have juices dripping off my chin. She quickly obeys without saying a word. She mounts me with her legs over my shoulders; only thing I see is her wet clit tempting me to suck it with brute force.

Pandora love sucking dick so her mouth had enough meat to keep her occupied for the moment. She twists my dick, going deeper and deeper down my shaft, and coming back up to lick the head.

Serenity grabs me by the back of my head and thrust her hip muscle in a sexy circular motion into my face. Her pussy is sliding from the bottom of my chin to my forehead.

She talks hardcore shit, "I want to feel that tongue in me. Eat my pussy like you love it. Make me cum right now, you fucking bastard."

It was an order and I was ready to be obedient by making her cum before invading her walls, licking through her labia like the last four corners on Earth. Slurping and biting on her flesh as she enjoys a pinch of pain with her clit in my mouth.

She uses her fingers and spreads it wider. My tongue is in a combat zone as I lick faster and grunt while eating her pussy. I want her to see that I eat pussy better than any woman including Pandora.

My dick is on the verge of exploding into Pandora's pit but I wait. I need her to beg like a dog for this nut. I pump her throat faster as I eat Serenity's pussy like a cannibal.

Serenity tells Pandora, "enough dick sucking" and she instantly stops.

Serenity leans back and continue fucking my face until her head was in my lap. She grinds everything into me as Pandora straddles her face.

I peek to watch but she pulls my head deeper into her hole until I couldn't see a thang.

Pandora whimpers," Make me cum!"

Her sexy ass voice turns me on so I add two more fingers into her pussy, she bucks and trembles.

"I'm cumming!" Pandora shouts.

My face was her Yellowstone Park as she shot a hot geyser all over me. I taste her juices on the tip of my tongue as the rest journey down my neck. I release her from my face to watch the remaining show.

Serenity screams," Fuck me hard! I want both of you to punish me until I lose my fucking mind."

Pandora runs to the other room and comes back with a strap on. This is the first time I have seen a woman with a fake dick but if they try some crazy shit, I'm going to fuck them up.

Serenity sees the look on my face and whispers, "Jerrod that's not for you but you should feel lucky that you are about to experience a barbaric fantasy."

Pandora came over and lied down on the couch as Serenity squatted over the dildo.

Serenity looks at me and say, "Now fuck me in my ass and don't stop until I cum all over this dildo."

I thought her hole would be tight but the juices from her pussy opened it up for easy access. She rides the dildo as I spread her cheeks with every inch.

She yells, "oh shit! I want it harder!'

I believe Pandora wants to have a contest to see who could fuck the best, plastic, or the real dick.

I can see the outer limits challenge from these two freaks in their eyes.

I choke Serenity, pounding this dick into her ass; looking at Pandora, I say, "come on, bitch, let me see what you got!"

Serenity is throwing that pussy and arching her back on my dick. She looks back and says, "You better hold that nut, you muthafucker."

I snarl like a vicious dog foaming at the mouth with one hand around her throat and the other one pulling her by the shoulders. I lift my ass, slam it back down; jumping in that ass like my dick was a trampoline.

"Tell that nigga whose dick is the best! Tell him Serenity and tell his ass right fucking now!" Pandora screams.

I look into her eyes and I see how much she enjoys fucking Serenity. At this moment, I know why some women love the lifestyle of being bisexual.

Serenity screams and humps the dildo as I keep thrusting into her soul. She yells, "I am about to cum, you fucking bastards. Please, don't stop! I'm begging you not to stop!"

I stroke my dick into deeper and harder as Pandora drives that dildo into her more. Serenity kisses Pandora with more fire and passion. I hear her pussy farting back with each stroke. I love that damn sound. Hell, I love being a part of this threesome.

Serenity breaks the kiss and says, "Aww. Aww, Aww, here I come!" She cums all over Pandora's leg. I know she was done, so I slides my dick out of her ass and push her on the floor.

Lifting up the dildo, I jump right in Pandora pussy, and throw her legs behind her head.

I fuck her hard, mainly because she never was this wild the whole time we were dating. Serenity finally came back up for air and squatted over Pandora face.

Pandora is licking while I am sticking her pussy. I want it to look like shredded meat by the time I pull this dick out.

"Eat this pussy, you little bitch. You're my bitch, fuck Jerrod," Serenity scream.

The more she tried to insult me, it made me punish Pandora more.

I keep up the pace and I am shocked that Serenity doesn't suffocate Pandora as she rides her face. Serenity plays with her clit, fingering her lips faster as I ram this dick all in Pandora.

I see the look on Serenity face as she releases another geyser over Pandora. I am beyond ready to explode myself so I pull my dick out and beat it as hard as I can.

Serenity lifts off Pandora face and begins kissing her juices off.

I tell them, "dinner is served. Taste this cumburger." They lick the tip of my head, back and forth.

"Feed us, you bitch!" they scream.

Any other time I would slap a hoe for talking shit to me but they deserve to be demanding.

I shake and feel the nut running through my vein as I unload on their faces. "Oh Shit!" I stagger a little but this nut is fucking outstanding.

I sit on the sofa with a limp dick. After that encounter, I want to go to sleep.

Serenity and Pandora kiss cum off each other lips. These freaks should make a porn tape with this X-rated shit for real.

"I knew you were tense with that nut backed up; you almost fainted trying to squeeze a round off," Serenity laughs.

The only thing I can do is smile besides she has a point. I'll never admit it but these ladies worked the shit out of me.

Serenity looks at me, "we are going to take a shower but if you have any more energy, round two will be in the bedroom."

She says, "There's Viagra on the nightstand just in case you need some help."

I tell her, "I can function without that bullshit. Keep your throat open like Motel 6."

The only thing I need energy for is to spend the money in my account tomorrow. I can live a stress-free life without worrying about Malakai or his smart-ass mouth bitch.

CHAPTER 28
ASPERILLA

"Pandora, where the hell have you been for the past month and why are you coming to see me?" I asks, "I almost had to kill a bitch last night for trying to touch my ass in the shower. Now I am talking through this phone like I am video chatting on Skype. I haven't heard from Malakai and this is the longest time we have been apart without communication."

"Asperilla, I know you are upset but please allow me to explain, Jerrod threatened me that if I went to the police, he would kill me. I didn't know he was going to drug your drink but I knew something was wrong when I saw that the police arrested you for the murder of Pastor Johnson. I am risking my life now being here but I had to wait until everything died down so I could come and visit. You have to believe me; we have been friends too long. So, what are the charges?" She inquires.

"Conspiracy to commit murder, and you know I am innocent of that bullshit. Someone is setting me up and if you are truly my friend, you would find out who is framing me." I snap.

"Asperilla, I have been out there looking and I stumbled upon the truth but I am not too sure if it will help you leave prison before your court date," she says.

"How the hell you know? Who told you that Jerrod drugged my drink? You were the only person that gave me one besides the bartender," I shouted. "Perra Traidora!"

"Yes, I did it and it felt damn good. By the way, I found Malakai, his ass is in a fucking morgue. Since you are always talking like you are the supreme diva then your ass can sit on the prison throne. I tried to wait as long as I could before dropping this news, but to be honest, you deserved it early. Treating me like I belong under your heels but today you have been served. So, you can break-dance your ass in your jail cell 'til eternity for all that I care," she confesses.

"They say a woman resorts back to her natural habitat when caged like an animal in the zoo. You ain't nothing but a Mexican spider monkey with a cute face," she says sarcastically. "Bitch, you make me sick. I am going to sit back and enjoy. Asperilla, I want you to meet someone that you know so well."

She motions for another person to come over to the visitation booth. This slut kisses her finger, touches the screen, hangs the phone down, and walks away. I can't believe Pandora has the audacity to talk shit but I'll take it for now. I'm going to pull her guts out with my bare hand when I see her on the outside. I couldn't finish my thoughts before the situation became more dramatic.

"Good afternoon Asperilla, I am so delighted that the police finally found my husband's killer. You almost ruined the best scam operation I had as the First Lady," she smirks. "Now, how does it feel to know that you are literally fucked? Speaking of the word fuck. How did it taste to have Pandora's pussy in your mouth while my juices were on your upper lips? Damn, I wish I could have ridden Malakai's dick one last time before he died because he loved to taste a good nut."

"Malakai is not dead!" I holler as I hit the screen with the phone. "You are dead when I get out this muthafucker!"

"Ms. Asperilla, you are really making a scene. Please calm down before they take away your visitation rights. There is a lot I want to say but a letter explaining everything will be delivered to add more fire. Now you can talk to your best friend or ex-girlfriend. To be honest, she has always been mine. I guess you can say I have taken everything you cared for in one month. Well, I have to leave and smile in front of the cameras. This visit was only to promote my new adventure by starring in my own reality show; plus, Lifetime wants to make a movie about me as the First Lady. I might even win a *Nobel Peace Prize* for my performance in the community. Well, baby, take care and since I am a forgiving woman, I will keep money on your books because I believe in blessing my enemies," she brags.

She exits the booth and Thing 2 comes scrolling along like she's floating on a cloud.

"Asperilla, Asperilla, Asperilla! I need one more look at your pitiful ass face before I walk away. That's enough. Time to go; when I go to the beach tomorrow, I'll make sure to play in the sun for you. Toodle-Loo," she laughs.

"Pandora, you do know this isn't the end of me, just remember that," I threaten.

She stands, tries to do my famous Dorothy heels clap, and hangs up the phone.

I held in a lot of emotions and it was extremely hard for me but the hurtful part is not knowing the truth about Malakai. I don't give a fuck if I have to break out of prison to kill those bitches and ring the doorbell to get back in; they will pay for this shit.

I signaled to the guard that my visit was over and he escorted me to my cell. He hands me a letter with the words *Love, the Punisher* written on the outside.

I know this letter is from Tasha's lunatic ass. If she wasn't such a retard, she probably could have pulled off the perfect crime. I know she has a lot of influential leaders behind her so that explains the charges without evidence. She would have been better off using a fucking donkey as an insider instead of Pandora's dried up ass.

I watch as he closes and locks the cell. I tell him thanks for the letter and I am truly anxious to read it. I rip the envelope open, slide the letter out, and read.

Dear Asperilla,

By the time you read this letter, your visitors have left you to relax in your luxury cell for the next 20 years. I regret not meeting you sooner because we could have ran this city together but then again, we probably would have bumped heads over supremacy. This letter is nothing personal but as you would say, this is just business. I take my role as the Punisher very seriously and you just happened to be in my lane as I rolled the ball. I do thank y'all for getting rid of Carlos. That was not the way I would have killed him but a body in the casket pays the same regardless of how it happens. I'll finish telling you more about me but let's chat a little about Pandora. Where do I start? Oh my. I met her when she danced at MONS VENUS, such a hell hole so I taught her how to save her money and go back to school.

Really amazing how she achieved her medical degree, truly proud of myself for that one because we both know that she is a piece of work at times. Yes! Pandora has been my woman for a long time so you and I are identical. We fuck over whomever just to make sure our cash flow never ends and we will die before going back to where we started. Let's see: the Pastor, well money and power can make you do terrible things.

I went to Bible College to blend in with those messy Christians. I had the perfect body and played the virgin role quite well and I became the illustrious First Lady. Carlos was a super whore so I had his office bugged to hear all of his conversations. It paid off with your little scheme with the photos; that was the greatest idea ever.

I must say that the sex during the morning service was such a turn on; if I could, I would have busted in and forced you to share Malakai's dick. Of course, you already know that I fucked him anyway; leftovers are just as good when they are reheated. Now as for Jerrod, I hooked him up with Pandora a year ago because he would do anything for money. He was a friend of Carlos' and Pandora needed to keep tabs on you. Now back to the most important part: yes, your drink was drugged by your friend, she had access to all kinds of pharmaceutical products. While you were in la-la land, we had the police to escort you from the boat to the jail. Being the First Lady that I am, it only took a few crooked cops to help plant the evidence. When they did the search at your home; they found the knife with Carlos's blood on it. Yes, I had some of his blood in a jar for about 4 months knowing it would come in handy and I have to thank you and that sexy ass poet. Now, today has come and I am about to become rich and known as the Mother Teresa of the 21st century. I could easily give up my work on speaking and teaching but ministry is the new prostitution. I will clean every soul dry and even lick the offering plate. Now back to Malakai, with his dead ass, let me spell it out for you: D-E-A-D. Last time I checked, his ass was pumped with enough lead to become a human pencil. Yes, and the only source of proving that you are innocent is gone and since you misused the escorts; they have turned their backs on you. I know you think I am stupid for writing this confession in a letter but I wanted you to taste a piece of pleasure since you believe in serving this city a lifetime of memories. Well, I am ending this with a smile but one more gift for you; I am sending in the guard to give you a special shakedown to destroy this letter, matter of fact, they should be ready to come in right about now.

Sincerely Yours,

The Punisher

When I looked up the guards were at my cell and there wasn't enough time to stash the letters. They come in without saying a word, flipping over things, screaming at the top of their lungs, and take the truth away from me.

I scream, "Get the fuck out!"

The cocky guard tells me, "Shut the hell up and enjoy your punishment for killing a man of God."

I know it's no use in fighting back so I stand to the side and watch them finish their shakedown.

Now that it is over, they say that they will be back in two days to make sure I am not hiding anything else.

I say, "Thanks for the customer service," while smiling like a Wal-Mart greeter.

Tasha and Pandora really are sniffing each other's pussies if they think I will sit behind these bars for the rest of my life.

I now understand why Malakai always trusted Ayanna and why he wanted us to become friends. If he is dead, then I have all the tools to seek justice on his behalf.

When it came down to spitting lines into people ears, Malakai was one of a kind. I would question him about tempting judges and lawyers into spending money with the escorts; I never was the type to play well with law enforcement but I need that ace of spade right about now.

I picked up everything the guards tossed. I see I am becoming the old Asperilla. I might rearrange this room so they can have another reason to be pissed at me. I am thinking about killing

Tasha and that thought alone almost makes me cum. I pat my pussy and say," Not now, baby, but I will have my orgasm when that bitch is screaming for her life. Now that's a nut I can savor."

CHAPTER 29

MALAKAI

I have never been to this poetry spot but the line is endless. The craziest thing is I am surrounded by people but unable to make out their faces. I am not sure how I arrived here but I know I want to bring the roof down here. As soon as I reach the door, I notice a sign that says, *No Erotic Poetry*. I think to myself that somebody's daughter will be missing out on an explosive eargasm. I finally reach the stage and it is made of pure gold with a diamond microphone glistening in the face of every person. I am astound by its beauty so I walk upon the stage to touch it when someone grabs my hand. I see a shirtless black man with dreads, built like a stallion. He had the war wounds to prove he was a soldier.

He looks at me and asks, "What makes you worthy to touch the mic of the Poetic God. You haven't earned enough strikes to bless my house. Who are you?"

I speak and say, "I am Mala" and before I could finish the "kai," he cuts me off saying, "You can't be the one preparing the way for me. You can't be the prophet to tell the world that when I come back, they will bow down and worship me when I speak.

"I am the Poetic Purifier, the Blazing Fire, and the Ultimate Judge. So, before you can come into my presence, what have you sacrificed in life to show that you love Me? I know you can't tell me because the real Malachi is over there; and you are only a copycat but created to be an original.

"Tell me: have you ever performed poetry in a lion's den, in a burning furnace, or enclosed by your enemies. You make a lot of noise but the best erotic poet to this day is not you but Solomon. Elijah come here!"

"Yes Lord! "Speaking with force, "Spit something for this bag of rags."

On Earth, I was considered the biblical troublemaker.
Anointed to pierce through people's hearts
And touch their souls like the creator.
So, when they told me to bow down
And worship another God,
I made Baal and the 450 prophets look like retards.
I challenge them to a slam.
Wasn't afraid of losing because I rep the Great I AM.
I open my mouth and made fire reign down from the sky.
My poetry burnt the bull, wood, stone and even the dust.
Slaughter the enemies and still to this today,
They still talk about us.

"That's enough Elijah. You can go back to your seat because he ain't ready for this poetic power. We physically spit in people's face to make them see. So, you have a prophet name but no purpose. I see that my gift inside of you has blessed your life tremendously.

"Now if you can stop being like your brother David and realize when you take advantage of a woman precious jewels, it's just as wrong as committing murder. I never did understand why certain men want to own or control a woman. I bless him to have one in the beginning and we all know how that story ended.

"Malakai, stand over there next to Moses and tonight your job is to listen to all the talent in heaven, the real *Poetic Heaven*. I might start collecting my royalty check from you since my inspiration is used as a club venue name."

I follow his instruction and enjoy the gifts of so many spirit-filled poets. Tears are flowing as the Poetic God spits a piece about love. The angels hum as His words strikes every verse with lightning. The room was silent until the last line. The crowd started snapping and clapping from his perfect poem.

"Malakai, spit a piece about revenge. If you want to bless this mic, then it needs to shift the atmosphere. Your heart is cold as ice and one day you will understand that revenge never brings joy or replaces what you lost. It only shifts it to the next person to act upon. I have watched you perform for years and one day, I will remove my love and gift from you."

I hear the crowd stomping their feet and chanting my name, "Malakai, Malakai, Malakai."

He says, "No need to waste the crowd's time, you want to seek your own justice. You better pray my mercy stays with you."

They chant my name louder, "Malakai! Malakai! Malakai!" My eyes slowly open and the first person I see in the room is Ayanna. I look for the Poetic God but he was nowhere to be found.

----------------ஓ ஓ ஓ ஓ ஓ ஓ---------------------

Ayanna says, "Welcome back to the land of the living."

"Thanks, but I felt like I died and gone to heaven; every time I close my eyes, I have the same dream," I explain.

"You are healing well but you lost a lot of blood and almost drowned at the pier. You are one lucky ass man or dude had a lousy aim. I thought you were dead by the time I made it there with the EMS and police. The paramedic said another ten minutes you would have choked on your own blood," she states.

"I am lucky those fools left me to die without double checking. Thank you so much for being there." I say with teary eyes.

"Quit being so damn sentimental. Anyway, I visited Asperilla two weeks ago. There is a lot that happened since the night of the incident," she smiles and speak.

"How is she?" I ask.

She puts her hand over my mouth and speaks, "Quit interrupting me and listen, she is alright. Tasha has played all of you for her political gains and on a mission to become some type of global icon."

"Damn, I didn't see that coming, I guess after fucking over so many women; one decided to fuck me," I speak surprisingly.

"Yeah, well it gets deeper. The night Asperilla went to the party was the beginning of the setup. Pandora invited Asperilla out so

214

she could drug her and have the crooked officers pick her up. She had been secretly dating Jerrod the whole time behind our backs. She reported everything we did to Tasha and Jerrod.

"They have been planning it since Carlos had sex adventures with the ladies. Pandora knew Asperilla would hit the panic code and they used that as an advantage to try and kill you," she expresses.

"Malakai, I'm glad that while you were in Houston, you thought beforehand for Asperilla and me to start working through our differences because I would have left her ass in prison to rot myself.

"Now back to this situation, the police were holding her on conspiracy to commit murder but with the newly found evidence, they have changed it to murder. Tasha has most of the city wrapped around her fingers. I can't believe how many people have bought into her bullshit. You should have seen her on TV last week promoting her new reality show.

"Asperilla is alright, just a little cranky about being in prison longer than expected. I can honestly say she truly loves you. She was talking about you during the visit. She even said that one day, she would trade in her wildlife and become a mother. I think it's that time alone in that cell and away from the beauty and nail shops that is invading her thoughts.

"I told her that you were alive. I have never seen her cry and can sense the emotions and anger wrapped up in her soul. I am visiting her next week to share the good news about your recovery," she admits.

"Ayanna, I fucked up bringing Love Divine with me. The saddest part is not being able to attend her funeral. How was it?" I ask with grief in my soul.

She cries, "All the ladies assisted with the funeral expenses and we held an all-star remembrance for her down at the club. I wish you could have seen it; all types of Poets came through to show their love and sympathy. She really was a woman with a heart of gold."

"Ayanna, thank you for telling me. I know it is my fault she lost her life. You know before I woke up, I had a dream that I was in Heaven and God was encouraging me to bless the mic with a piece titled *Revenge and Forgiveness*; I know I have done some awful things but Jerrod will pay for everything.

"To make matters worse, I even begged him to let her go. He pulled out a knife and cut her throat. I saw as he slit her flesh from her right ear to her left. My heart dropped as her body fell. I should have left her at the club with her friends; maybe she would be alive today.

"When you visit Asperilla tell her that I am ok and I will get her out before she breaks out. You know she doesn't have it all and Pandora should have thought twice before crossing Asperilla. She is probably creating her own version of 1,000 ways to die.

"If Tasha and her goons think I am dead, then let's give them what they want. She thinks she has the upper hand because her husband was a prominent man in the community and can ride his coat tail. I am about to tear down her kingdom like the Walls of Jericho."

"FRIENDSHIP AND BONDING ARE
WONDERFUL UNTIL ONE DISAPPEARS, LEAVING
ONLY SAD MEMORIES AND GRAY SKIES
BEHIND."

CHAPTER 30

MALAKAI

After four long months, I am able to function normally. I walk to the bathroom and wash my face and notice my wounds are healing quickly. I am so angry right now. I want to kill Tasha but jail is the last thing I need to see. I am going to write and perform a poem one day about Deadly Patience so they will always remember the day Malakai was left for dead.

I haven't called Kryptonite to tell him that I am alive. The city thinks I am dead and it is the only way to play this perfect plot. I am thankful for pussy but with money and drugs, you can't imagine national connections.

Asperilla will be out of jail by the end of the week and the business meeting with the ladies will be this weekend. In the beginning, a lot of fools used to ask what the purpose was of treating your escorts like royalty. My response will forever be that they are loyal and willing to lay their life down for me.

I walk out of the bathroom, open the balcony window, and inhale the fresh air. This is a beautiful getaway place. I am secretly living in the house since I left the hospital. Tasha pulled one of my numbers by paying off a few officers. I am blessed to have one I can trust on my team. She took me to the hospital, cleaned up the mess on the pier and kept the media out of my business. I close the door and walk downstairs to watch T.V. I flip through a few channels and see Tasha's conniving ass with her own reality show.

I want to punch the screen but I decided to watch and learn her daily moves. She is giving me a road map to her funeral.

After gaining knowledge on her daily activities, I know I need a close friend to do my work and follow Jerrod. I pick up the cell and dial Undercover Brothers. I always hated that name for a private investigator's agency; it has been their family name for a few generations but they are the best.

He answers, "Malakai, is that you? Man, I knew you were alive because there is no way you would go out like that."

I tell him, "It was close. I'm breathing but fuck all of that; can you do a favor for me? I need you to do a little background check on this guy named Jerrod; he is a friend of Carlos and Tasha."

He laughs, "I will have the information by the close of business tomorrow."

I told him thanks and hang up the phone. I am contemplating seeing Divine's memorial site. This is a hard pill to swallow knowing that I am responsible for her death. No matter how much pain I inflict on Tasha and them, it will never bring back her smile and voice. I will live with this pain for the rest of my life.

I grab my keys and drive to the cemetery. It is really hard trying to be incognito when you are a famous poet but I am still a country boy at heart so I can blend in with a chameleon on any day. I have been hiding in Land O' Lakes and this is the first time that I am driving back to the city since that fatal night.

The interstate is moving freely and it only takes me 45 minutes to reach my destination. I park, walk towards her memorial and place a Poinsettia on her tombstone.

I used to think that I was extremely popular but this woman had the power to move mountains whenever she spoke. I will always love how her stage presence demanded attention. Reminiscing over those moments brings tears to my eyes. I know if she was here, she would probably call me a big ass sissy. She would say, *you are a pussy poet for crying over a woman. What the hell is wrong with you?*

A smile comes to my face as I hear her voice inside of my head, knowing her memories will forever have a special place in my heart. I am having a conversation with her and I feel a little silly but I know she hears me in heaven.

I tell her, "The day we met, God opened the doors of heaven to bless me. You were more than an Angel but a woman that any man could worship. It was truly an honor to be a part of your world by sharing a poetic chemistry together that could ignite an explosion.

"You have taught me that true friendship and love are precious gifts to cherish daily. Your name means everything to me; it's amazing that we shared the same birthday. Yes, Gemini's created to be forever lyrically joined at the hip. Forever. I miss everything about your hair, skin tone, and smile.

"I need you. I pray you will find it in your heart to forgive me since I wasn't there to protect you. I want you to know that I will always love you for giving strength to those even in your weakness.

"I owe you so much and I promise that your name will not be in vain. I had been living on the edge for a long time and had forgotten who I was before you. I always wanted fame, money, and pussy but meeting you was the friendship that I needed to prosper into my new destiny."

At that moment I felt a strong wind blowing over me and I know it is her telling me to respect her memorial and stop using so much profanity. "Okay I hear you; sorry about that one. Now where was I. Oh Yeah! I miss you so much and there will never be another poet like you. I will continue on helping people and giving poetry my all.

"I think I am going to change the name of my club to Love Divine because you are a piece of Poetic Heaven. I will forever cherish our collab and thank you for allowing me to be a part of your Divine Love.

"Well, it wouldn't be me if I didn't say a small piece before I leave so if you are ready, here I go..."

Love is the greatest gift in the universe.
So, allow me to free-verse
This piece with no rehearses to say Divine I thank you
For being my emotional nurse.
Caring for my heart with nothing in return.
Even when I felt alone,

You always showed me that you were concerned.
You are a friend that can transcend dreams
Into reality blessings.
I know you are a part of God.
When you speak, I can feel His heart.
My life was possessed with stress until you taught me
How to sweep away my mess.
I will never walk like you but I can strive to be
Everything that you have taught me.
To never speak negative and always believe
That I can do all things.
Through Christ who strengthens me.
I love you.

"So, what do you think? I swear I hear your voice telling me not to do another wack piece over your memorial. I promise to always visit you and I'll bring a picnic basket next time."

Yeah, imagine people walking by and I am having a beautiful afternoon lunch with a woman that is so Divine.

"I want you to know that I have stopped chasing pussy but I will forever chase this dick down their ears, believe that.

"Well, I am going to leave but thank you for everything and I know God will give you the opportunity to rock heaven's mic. I pray that I see you perform up there as well. Take care, my friend." I get up, dust off my pants, walk to my car, and start the engine.

Playing on the radio is *Soul Heaven* by Johnny Taylor. This has to be a sign that everything will be alright as I sing along with JT.

There was a party in Soul Heaven
Superstars from the past
Standing room only, so you better hurry
Buy your ticket cause they're going fast.

CHAPTER 31

ASPERILLA

The foreman stood and stated, "We the jury find the defendant, Asperilla Valdez, not guilty of first-degree murder in the death of Carlos Johnson."

I knew those bogus charges couldn't hold me so I gave my lawyer a hug and big kiss. I have the perfect defense team in my corner. Once Malakai sent my lawyer the video of the man breaking into our home to plant evidence, they had no other choice but to free me. It is very ironic that the same man on the video was the officer trashing my cell every night. I believe someone will be trashing his ass on a nightly basis now.

I decided to show the world how you walk out of the courtroom in a pair of silver Jimmy Choo stilettos. I leave stardust on the floor as I take my new steps to freedom. It wouldn't be an Asperilla moment if I didn't piss a few people off so I blew a kiss at the prosecutor, twirled my fingers around in the air, and wipe my tongue. I slowly whisper so he could read my lips, "suck my chocha." I knew it would set him off at the right moment because he threw all of his paperwork on the floor as I walk past him.

It seems that every news reporter in Tampa was waiting outside to interview me. I politely tell them, "no comment at this time," but they keep coming toward me. I am doing my whoosah technique so I wouldn't have to hurt someone and end up right back in jail. I smiled and snatched the microphone out of her hand.

"So, you want to know how it feels to be framed for a murder you didn't commit?" Before I could answer her question, a purple Bentley pulls up and blows the horn. I toss the microphone to the woman and run to the curb. I open the door, jump in, and ask what took you so damn long to come and get me.

He drives off without saying a word and it causes my pussy to leak through the car seats. I want to fuck but I need to teach his ass a lesson for making me wait.

It's a wonderful thing this car has some dark tint and if it didn't, I will suck his dick in broad daylight inside of a convertible. I unfasten my seatbelt and run my fingers up his neck and down his chest.

I can't believe he is actually driving and trying to ignore me; no kiss, no I miss you, no nothing.

I slowly unzip his pants and pull his dick out. I could feel it stretching out in my hand and becoming erect.

I flicker my tongue across his head real slowly and he loves when I spit on it. I think it turns him on since he's a poet. I move my head to the song on the radio and he grinds his hips with my mouth. We are in sync as he enters the interstate to take us home. I know he wants to say something and in a minute he will. I glide my tongue down his dick, up and down with a faster tempo. I keep that up for two minutes and it was driving him crazy.

I come back up and slam my throat muscle back down. My head game is like manslaughter because I slaughter and swallow his dick to pieces. I look up and see him clutching the steering wheel tighter and he is winding his hips like a Jamaican. He opens his mouth and moans, "damn, I missed you so fucking much." I know I have his ass in the right spot so I open my mouth and bite his dick so fucking hard until he swerves off the interstate.

He pulls over to the shoulder to regain his composure and he is pissed as hell.

He screams, "What the fuck is wrong with your crazy ass?"

I smear his precum on my lips like gloss, and say, "that's for not getting me out of jail fast enough. I really thought you were dead when that bitch came down there talking shit.

"Malakai, I love you and spending so much time in that cell only made me realize that I want to spend the rest of my days making you happy."

He yells, "You have a funny way of showing it, by trying to Lorena Bobbitt my shit!"

Sensually, I say, "I promise to make you feel like a King and my royal chamber is ready for your scepter. You can deposit your riches in all of my holes."

He says, "You are a fucking retard but I will play your game." Then he asks, "How did you figure out that Tasha was the one responsible for orchestrating the devious plot."

I explain, "The first night the detectives questioned me is when I retraced my steps. I asked myself who had the most to lose because of the Pastor death but receive more from it at the same time. Then it hit me, the First Lady was playing us from day one.

"She knew we were the ones fucking that morning in the Pastor's office during the sermon. She knew her husband was fucking Cherry and other girls; what black woman you know, Christian or not, would take that news so damn easy without getting even?

"That bitch was on TV with fake tears and quoting scriptures. I knew Pandora had broken up with another woman when we met years ago at the club but the name Serenity didn't ring a bell until they visited me four months ago. I wouldn't have suspected Tasha either but her plan was damn near perfect. She tried to frame me for the crime, murder you, and cash in the sympathy checks as she walks around portraying Michelle Obama.

"I probably would have done the same thing except I wouldn't have used Pandora and Jerrod unless they were expendable. I am so sorry to hear about what happened with Love Divine because you were trying to save me. I had no idea that Pandora was going to set me up but after I felt the effects of the drugs, I called you immediately."

I see mentioning her name struck his heart deep but he looks at me and says, "no worries because judgment is coming."

We finally pull up to the driveway and it is so nice to be home.

I ask, "How long are you going to fake your death since you pulled a risky move picking me up?"

He responds, "Just long enough to take out Jerrod and Pandora, disrupt Tasha's Women Empowerment Conference and turn all of her dreams into nightmares in one day."

The conversation was a beautiful one. He exits the car, walks to my side and opens the door. He extends his hand and I quickly accept his invitation. He picks me up, carries me into the house and I hear the soft music playing.

I ask, "What are you up to?"

He replies, "Something that we haven't done in a long time." I am a little nervous but I am willing to play my role.

He unbuttons my suit jacket and pulls it off real slow. He drops to my ankles and slides off my shoes like I am Cinderella. He looks up and I gaze into his eyes with intense passion. He takes off my pants and I shake my hips so my pants come down with ease.

I am standing in the middle of the room in my lace lingerie in one of his favorite colors, candy red. He presses his lips and parts my mouth to tongue wrestle. I feel his fingers trailing down my back and landing on my ass, squeezing my cheeks.

I feel his tongue deeper in my mouth and its making the juices drench throughout my boy shorts.

He lies me down and says, "I want you to rinse my face like a washing machine and leave these boy shorts on."

I see my legs go up like an escalator and immediately wrap them around his neck.

He licks my pussy through my boy shorts and I feel his tongue traveling to my canal. He slowly pulls them to the side and introduces two fingers into my chambers. I moan sweet pleasure as my thighs squeeze tighter around his head.

He digs his fingers in and is immediately soaked in my juices; this shit has my head spinning in circles. I haven't had a good squirt in a long time so this will not take long.

I scream, "Malakai, I love your tongue! Please, suck my clit harder!"

He listens and obeys without missing a beat as I stroke his face with my pussy. I grabbed his head to let my juices flow in his nose and out of his mouth. He keeps feasting regardless if I drown him or not. I feel his tongue blowing through me like a tidal wave every fucking time he slams it against my shores.

He never ate my pussy with so much finesse. I hear his tongue lapping at me quicker as he inserts another finger inside of me. The third finger, with his devastating tongue, is all I need as tears run down my face. I don't know if I want to push him off or catch this nut. This is some emotional shit right now and I am scared and aroused at the same time.

I scream, "I am about to cum! Oh shit!"

I can feel the moisture running between my lips. If I was Fred Sanford, I would say, *Elizabeth I am coming to join ya, because this is the big one.*

I never had the pleasure of wiping away tears before an orgasm until now but it seems like everything is running out of me. I look down one last time and see him pulling out his dick.

He strokes his shaft with his right hand, using the left to open my pussy wider as I pull his face deeper into my pussy. I hear the grunting sounds he makes while beating his dick. I am turned on harder than ever; I push like I am having a baby and I squirt down his face and he keeps eating. Damn, his ass refuse to take a break as I shake, scream, and tries to push him away.

He finally stops, stands, and ejaculates all over my lace boy shorts. He is back on his knees and I am thinking not right now; shit, I think I broke something. I watch as he reaches inside of his pocket and pulls out a three-carat diamond ring.

He looks at me and says, "Asperilla, will you marry me?"

I thought about everything that we have been through and I knew that my life wouldn't be complete without him. I scream, "Yes!"

He gives me the biggest hug and slips the ring on my finger. I know that I have been a shady woman but it's incredible how he has the power to forgive and want me to be his wife. The victory in court today couldn't compare to the high that I am on right now.

I kiss him over and over until he stops, looks at me, and says, "You continue looking at your ring. I'm about to rip these boy shorts off to propose to my pussy."

"GET ON YOUR KNEES AND PROPOSE WHILE CUM RUNS DOWN YOUR NOSE. THAT WAY, YOU KNOCK OUT THE ENGAGEMENT AND HER ORGASM AT THE SAME TIME."

CHAPTER 32

MALAKAI

"Good evening, ladies, I know it has been a long time since I have called a meeting but this one is extremely important. First of all, let me thank all of you for helping Love Divine's family with the funeral and also establishing a college scholarship in her memory.

"I promise not to take up too much of your time tonight but we have to establish a game plan to take out Jerrod. I know he is still in the streets talking about how he left me for dead and bragging about assaulting Cherry. I also know he is still sniffing between legs and lusting for a sexual challenge. We will provide him with that opportunity next weekend.

"Ayanna, Cherry, and Jaz, please let me know if you are up for this fuck mission and if not, I'll resort to Plan B," I direct.

They agree in unison and I am very surprised Jaz is so eager to set up a man.

I ask Jaz, "For a woman making her way into the game, why are you so anxious to help kill this man?"

She responds, "My life in Houston was boring as fuck and being around ya'll is an action movie that never ends. I am young, dangerous, and skillful; besides, the money is incredible."

I believe I have created an Asperilla Junior and that is scary but she is loyal to the family.

I tell her," I will pay you the most since I am putting you on the front line."

She stands, dances and shouts," Mo Money, Mo Money," while twerking.

Everyone laughs and it brings a smile to my face.

I tell them, "Okay, now, all jokes aside; let's get back down to executing this plan. We are about to hit Jerrod's ass like the Navy Seals that took out Bin Laden. I know he likes to hang out with the hood crowds and he will be partying this weekend at Club Underground, so Jaz, I know you can blend in nicely. Ayanna, you have to return to your Georgia Peach ways for one night and rep that dirty south."

Ayanna quickly replies, "Just because I am about to retire and become a professional, doesn't mean I have lost my ATL flava."

I love when she defends her hometown and I know all I have to do is sit and wait for them to pull his ass out of the club.

They say, "This will be a piece of cake and no need to worry about us fucking up anything".

I look at Cherry and I know she wants to be a part of the action and say, "just relax, you will have your payback plus a whole lot more."

We are a family and this kill is for Love Divine; we make a toast in her honor.

I finished talking about the plan when Asperilla came into the room and you can hear a pen drop. I can feel the tension but I know she has something to get off her chest. The first person that she looks at is Cherry, and she didn't want to seem weak but she actually says the F-word.

She says, "Cherry, I am truly sorry for mistreating you. Karma is a bitch and I shouldn't have had you sexing the preacher for my own financial gain. I am responsible for a lot of things that have happened to you this past year. I want to take this time to ask for your forgiveness and the only way I can make things right is to kill one of the monsters that tried to destroy our empire."

I look at Cherry and she quickly tells Asperilla, "it's not the end of the world; we all have done crazy things. Sleeping with the Pastor was awesome because he could really fuck." She screams, "Hell yeah, I forgive you! Besides, it will be too boring around this place if you kept being so nice to me."

Asperilla looks at me and says, "I know you all are planning Jerrod death but Pandora belongs to me and only me. I am going to kick in her front door, pull out her teeth, and then cut off her nipples for fun."

I know she is going to enjoy her revenge like a serial killer has a work of art. She walks out of the room with a twisted smile.

She makes it to the door, looks back and says, "You all can continue. I'll be back in five minutes."

I kept talking until I notice out the corner of my eye that Asperilla was walking back in the room with a machete.

She says, "When I was a kid, my uncle once chopped the hands off a man stealing money; I will never forget that day," she says as she hands the machete to me. "Malakai, please do me the honors of bringing Jerrod head in a box so I can deliver it to Pandora."

The ladies say, "We want the old Asperilla back. Shit just got real."

I tell her, "as long as there is breath in my soul, your wish is my command."

Ayanna asks, "What are we going to do about Tasha?" I knew that question would come up eventually.

I tell Ayanna, "The First Lady's reality show is about to go viral."

I say to the ladies," I will contact some friends about attending the Women's conference to make sure she doesn't escape. I know she will have someone protecting her all day so we need a big distraction and everything will be flawless. I will call ya'll tomorrow so enjoy a no client week. I need you all to be well rested by next Saturday." They agree and exit the room, laughing and joking.

I think to myself that the world has never enjoyed the taste of loyal pussy until they have licked the ones from our stable. If I had a way to clone them then I would be able to spin this whole city in reverse.

I hear Asperilla in the kitchen talking shit, "You are better than me when it comes to Jerrod; I would hire a South American shemale."

I didn't want to ask her why in the world I would need someone like that.

She tells me, "just in case he tries to bully Jaz around; you could have a woman with breasts and ass but packs a dick." She is telling wild stories about certain guys that were bringing in more money than the female's prostitute.

"Asperilla, I don't have time for your wild out escapades. Plus, Jaz will be superb with this mission. I know she has what it takes to force him out of the club and back to the house. The more he drinks, the less he will be able to stand on his own. I will make sure Ayanna is at the club because this fucker lives for a threesome," I explain.

I look at Asperilla, ask her to sit on my lap and she comes with no hesitation. I caress her back and say everything will be alright in a few months.

I tell her, "We have been in this pussy game so long and deep that it's hard to pull out."

She laughs and says," trust me, we will put our legs down after we bust the biggest nut and then we can retire."

I smile and say, "You are so beautiful and I can't wait to marry you. It has truly been a long evening and I just want to hold you until the sun rise."

She asks while twirling her hair, "is that all you going to do?"

I answer, "Maybe I will leave my eyes between your thighs so when you need me, I can always see you cumming."

We laugh and go upstairs with happiness and anticipation of next weekend.

"BE CAREFUL WHO YOU NUT IN. NOT
EVERYONE DESERVES YOUR POWERS."

CHAPTER 33

AYANNA

We arrived at the club and the line was super long but Malakai contacted the bouncer earlier so he let us in as VIP for tonight. They weren't lying about how ratchet this place is but the crowd is turnt up and the bartenders are working their ass off.

Jaz looks at me and ask, "Do you see Jerrod?"

I respond, "this place is huge, we can't go looking for him so the men will come to us."

She says, "What do you mean, Ayanna?"

"Tonight is a twerk battle and I am going to enter you as Alexis," I inform her.

Jaz yells, "you gonna do what?"

I mischievously say, "Yeah girl. Mine is Honey and this shit is going to be epic. The way you took that guy's money in Ybor City; I want you to do the same shit here. We will show these hooded up muthafuckers so relax, I will be right back; I need to get some reinforcements."

I leave Jaz, walk to the DJ, and sign our names. I figure what the fuck since I am leaving the game, I might as well show these Floridians how a Georgia Peach can suck up the night. I texted the escorts I invited to party with us.

I stand by the booth as they walk in; only the perfect ones to turn heads. I have Asians, Puerto Ricans, Canadians, Caribbean and some sexy white girls to bring in that vanilla flavor. They are making their presence known by throwing ass with every step with heels, hats, and tight dresses. I met them in the middle and we walked towards the VIP booth.

Jaz shows her gratitude by giving them hugs for hanging out with us.

I tell them, "Look, y'all are here to cheer as we show the Underground how to Chop and Screw."

We laughed and I motioned for the waiter to bring the finest wine at the bar. Tonight is young and we need to unwind from sucking and fucking.

I know I will need some dick after we finish this wild ass night. We are joking and talking for about an hour until the DJ spins the last song.

He announces, "The twerk contest will begin in 10 minutes and we need all the ladies to report to the dance floor."

I grabbed Jaz's hand, raced to the floor, stood beside her and told her that we got this. They can't fuck with us; just let the wildness come out. She smiles and says the crown is coming back to the VIP section tonight.

The DJ says, "Tonight, we are going to do something a little different. We will always have a twerk battle but someone wrote on the sign-up list that they are willing to pay $2,500 dollars to dance against a woman by the name of Alexis."

Jaz eyebrows raised 10 feet when he said her name. I laughed knowing that I was responsible for this.

"Ladies, you can still twerk but please stand to the side because this is a personal dance off. The winner has also noted that I can claim half of the prize so you know it's going down tonight. Dancing against Alexis is a sexy delicious Georgia peach who goes by the name of Honey."

The crowd cheer and Jaz says, "You are dirty as hell but I am going to bust your ass for making up those crazy ass names."

The DJ says, "I will flip a coin to see who gets the chance to pick the song. Heads or Tails, call it in the air."

Jaz calls out, "Heads," as it goes in the air and lands in the DJ hand.

He looks down and asks, "Tails, Honey the song is yours. What would you like to hear?"

"I think I will go old school with *Shake That Ass Bitch* by Splack Pack," I say noticing the DJ wasn't ready for that one. Hell, this new generation knows nothing about real booty music.

The DJ says, "I guess we are going back in time."

I glance at Jaz and say, "I am about to scrub the floor with your ass. Nothing personal, just business."

The DJ says, "This is the rule. You have only one song to dance to and the audience will decide the winner. Underground! It's time to shake some ass."

Jaz hits the floor like a grasshopper while bouncing her ass without missing a beat and the crowd was like, "Damn!"

I twirl my hips, grab the first guy and throw him on the floor. I ride my pussy on his face and I did my 360 twerk all over his head.

Jaz knows she is in trouble. She pulls a guy out the crowd and out of all the guys in the club this one is with his woman. One thing about Jaz, she is so sexy that the woman dances on her.

I hear the DJ shouting, "1 minute left."

I twerk towards the top of his head and this idiot is just lying there. It's a good thing I took gymnastics in high school; I do a handstand, jiggle my booty cheeks left to right, and I land hard as I could on top of his chest. The crowd was like, "what the fuck!"

Jaz takes the couple down to the ground, jumps in the air and does a split on top of them. We are twerking on top of our victims until the DJ screams time is up.

He is shocked as fuck, mostly because who dance like this in dresses. When you are a member of the baddest escorts on the planet, you create shit that will implant memories in their mind.

We feel like we left the gym but all the eyes in the club are on us. I hear the crowd screaming, "One more song, one more song."

The DJ announces, "We can't take all of this in too many dosages so they will have to return another night. Now Underground, who deserves to go home with the crown?"

I know it will be a hard choice. Jaz will probably win but I am surprised when the cheers are almost equal.

The DJ call us on the stage, waves his hand over us and the crowd keeps cheering, "more, more, more," so he says fuck this, I'm calling this one a tie and the crowd goes into an uproar.

I smile at Jaz and say, "it's time to go back to the booth since part one is successful and now it's time to find Jerrod's punk ass."

We walked to the booth; all the ladies congratulated us on shutting the Underground down.

I look at them and say, "Thanks but I need to soak these bones later because Jaz almost wore my ass out."

Jaz smiles and says, "I had no idea that you could move like that. You almost had me when you hit that handstand so I had to think of something quick because I'll be damned if you were going to out dance me."

I laugh and say, "We can battle another day".

A man's voice interrupts me, "both of you can battle me tonight."

The plan worked like a charm, I saw Jerrod and his goons standing by the booth. I look at him up and down and immediately see nothing but an arrogant thug. I can't stand a grown ass man that never pulls his pants up. How the hell you are thirty-something but still dress like you're thirteen? I have no idea how these ladies can date men like that. What can he possibly teach your kids, how to play Call of Duty?

He flashes his grill and says, "Ladies, I really enjoyed the show and I personally want to invite you to our VIP section."

I think to myself; we aren't groupies and I have my own booth but this is for Love Divine and Malakai.

I give the fakest but cutest smile and say, "give us 10 minutes and we will be right over there."

The other ladies laugh because they know he isn't our type of client or a person we would ever date.

I tell the ladies, "enjoy the evening."

They respond, "Hell, we are on our way to the Blue Martini as soon as you seal the deal."

I whisper to Jaz, "It's time for phase two and we will work this nigga out of his socks."

She gives me the *I'm down for whatever look* and we walk over to his booth. Malakai will pay extra because the smoke in this place is too much for me.

He tries to show off in front of his little entourage saying, "Told ya'll that I could get them to come over so pay me my money right now."

The other ladies in the booth keep eyeballing us like they had X-ray vision or something.

I kiss Jaz to give them something to talk about. The fellas scream, "Damn, we got some sexy freaks in this bitch!"

Jerrod tells them, "settle down. They are leaving with me."

I correct him and say, "no, you are leaving with us real soon because we don't like to masturbate alone."

I guess that is the only thing this horny bastard needs to hear. He quickly pounds up his partners and say, "I will be leaving shortly."

We talk with his crew but I remember how they drugged Asperilla so whenever they offer us a drink, I quickly reply, "We are only drinking nuts on the rocks tonight."

His entourage laugh and say, "Jerrod, you are one lucky bastard."

I say, "Excuse me, Jerrod. Are you going to play with these hard legs all night or play in our pussies?"

I could tell that I struck his little ego because he stood up, threw some money on the table, and told his friends that should cover the tab.

He looks at us and answers, "ladies, this dick is all yours for tonight," then he walks us out the door.

I immediately answers, "You talk a lot of shit but let's see if you are man enough to talk when you have a mouth full of pussy. You can follow us home."

He didn't waste a second as he points to his car and says, "I'll be right behind ya'll."

We walk to the car and I tell Jaz to call Malakai because there is a change of plans since I don't trust this nigga. She explains the plot and I overhear him agreeing to my plans.

We leave the club and head straight to the house.

Jaz complains, "This idiot has my clothes smelling like weed. If I don't change, I will be high off the scent."

I tell her, "It's ok because tonight is the last blunt this nigga rolls."

We arrive at the house; he pulls behind us and honks the horn to let us know he is ready. We exited the car and walked up the driveway. It's a good thing that Malakai chose a house where the neighbors minded their business.

We reach the front door and Jerrod is still talking shit about how he is going to fuck me in the ass and make Jaz suck his dick. I think to myself that his breath smells like shit and this muthafucker is talking with every step.

I stick my key in the hole and tell him, "Welcome to Paradise."

He brags, "Yeah. Thanks, but I'm about to relax this dick in ya'll bitches mouths. Let me piss first and I will save a drop for ya'll to sip on."

He walks to the bathroom, opens it and almost shits on himself.

CHAPTER 34

MALAKAI

"Good morning, Jerrod. You act like you saw a ghost or something. No need to say anything because I want you to be quiet just like the silencer on this Glock. I won't entertain you long tonight but let's go back to the night on the pier. Remember you told me, since I love pussy so much, I can die by a piece of pussy? It is very ironic that your lust for power and your hungry dick have caused your downfall. The only difference between me and you is that I am going to make sure you never harm a woman again," I proudly reveal.

He yells, "Fuck you, Malakai! I bet you wouldn't be talking that shit without that pistol."

"You are probably right but that is something you will never know. Take your gun out nice and slow. If you try something stupid, I promise to unload every shot into your head. You should have killed me your damn self."

He obeys and slowly tosses the pistol to the side. I whisper, "You are about to meet an old friend."

He laughs and says, "I am about this life and ain't afraid to die."

I say, "Well, that's good news because I ain't afraid to kill."

The front door opens and Cherry walks in carrying an Indian War Club.

He smiles and says, "I guess you didn't enjoy the last beating I gave you."

He didn't have chance to finish his smile when the club connects with his skull. He hits the ground and she keeps wailing on him with blows.

I tell Cherry, "Don't fuck up his face."

She beats on his legs and arms; I can tell that she enjoys bashing his ass so I let her go to war on his soul.

I look at Jaz and Ayanna and say, "you all are free to leave," but they decide to stay and watch.

I say to Cherry, "stop for a minute so we can torture his ass until he begs to be put out of his misery."

I grab the handcuffs off the sink. I look at Cherry and say, "cuff them around his back."

She didn't waste any time because she cuffed him then finished beating him.

She screams, "You ain't talking shit now, you fucking coward."

I see the blood splatting from each blow and I know his bones are crackling.

He finally sees that this won't end any time soon.

He begs and says, "I am sorry for killing that girl. Tasha made me do it; I swear it's all her fault. Please, let me go and I won't say anything."

"Jerrod, you are so full of shit. I already know that you were friends with Carlos so you attacked Cherry to get even. You and Tasha should have let the naughty Pastor rest in peace and maybe everything would have been alright. To be honest, it doesn't matter whose idea it was to kill my friend, frame my woman, and take me out. I am going to make sure you all burn in hell before this year is out.

"I really want to beat your ass; I don't want to take the pleasure from Cherry but trust and believe I will revenge Love Divine before the night is over," I admit.

I signal Cherry to finish; she jumps up with excitement like I gave her a free pass to Universal Studios or something.

She swings that club like Barry Bonds and he screams louder and louder. I tell her to work every part of his body and don't miss shit. I pulled up a seat to enjoy the show. She strikes his shins first and I know she busted them bitches open. She is in heaven and slowly working her way to his kneecaps.

I vow, "Every blow you swing is for Love Divine and her family."

She strikes his kneecaps until they bleed and shatter.

I yell, "I don't even want this muthafucker to walk, cripple his ass."

I look at Ayanna and ask, "are you sure you want to watch this because it is about to get gruesome?"

She shakes her head and says, "Yes!"

Jaz smiles. Damn, I swear I hired a psycho from Texas.

Cherry is tired as hell from swinging so she decides to take a break.

Jaz looks at me and asks, "Can I play while she rests?"

"Feel free to batter up," I say.

She opens his legs and swings 5 blows into his nuts.

I braced myself because I didn't see that one coming. She keeps swinging nonstop until I grab her and say, "Damn, Jaz. That's enough!"

I can tell that he is barely alive and the meat on his skin is changing colors.

I ask Cherry, "are you done with your revenge or do you want more?"

She looks at me and say, "Malakai, my dad uses to abuse me and I told myself I would kill any man that ever laid a hand on me. As a matter of fact, this is his club that I brought with me when I came to Florida. I am going to beat him until shit runs out of his ass."

She kicks him in his stomach and beats his back. I stopped counting after 20 and walked out the room. His ass isn't going to move or fight back. I tell Ayanna and Jaz to follow me outside to talk about the evening.

Jaz says, "That club was ghetto and I pray I never have to go back."

Ayanna agrees, "Yeah, it was a fucked-up spot but it was worth getting Jerrod." The weed smell is not coming out of their clothes so they need some new outfits.

I laugh and say, "If I wasn't faking my death, I would have snatched his ass from his house but I cannot blow this cover until I catch Tasha at the right moment. I am envious of Cherry right now because she is getting her revenge and loving it."

We talked 15 more minutes about the business and their extra pay.

They ask, "How long do you plan on staying in the game?"

I smile and say, "You never know since the club is growing and honestly, we can leave at any time but the connection we have made is worth so much more. I have a few Army generals that want to work with us. You know that they're some freaky muthafuckers in the military," as we head back to the house.

We walk in and Cherry is sitting in the chair dripping with sweat and blood. I asked if she was okay and it took her a minute to answer because she had beaten Jerrod 'til she was out of breath. She did better than I expected.

I tell her, "I have to dispose of his body because I can't leave any evidence behind for the police to find."

She agrees and gives it to me with no problem.

I command Ayanna, "take some of the ladies to the beach condo and clean up there instead of going home."

I will have the maid clean up everything tomorrow. She probably will think I fucked a woman on her period again; damn, I'm so proud that I have changed.

I gather everything that I have and tell them that I will meet them by the car in about 10 minutes. I pull out Asperilla's machete, cut off Jerrod head, and whisper into his ear, "This is for Love Divine."

I giftwrap it in a box as she requested because Asperilla is dead ass serious about delivering it to Pandora as a birthday present. I think to myself, it's never a dull moment with the ladies I date.

I go to my car, grab the gasoline cans, and head back inside. Pouring gasoline throughout the whole house to make up for the tears shed for Love Divine until the cans are bone dry.

I put it in my car and prepared to do the best part of the night.

Ayanna asks in shock, "Are you really going to give Asperilla his head?"

I snap, "Hell yea!"

She asks again, "Why did you bring us here and whose house are you about to torch?"

I admit, "This is one of the Pastor's old homes that is barely used but Tasha's name is still on the mortgage. If Jerrod was about that life he would have known that."

I tell them to load everyone in the car and leave. I look around and know this neighborhood was perfect. It's dark, secluded and these old folks ain't about to say anything as long as you leave them alone.

I walk to the door and spread some of Tasha illegal financial records over the front lawn and throughout the room by the front door. I pull out some matches and start a fire in the living room and walk out.

It didn't take long for the gasoline to blaze the house; I didn't even look back.

CHAPTER 35

PANDORA

I know Asperilla is lurking around this city somewhere. I tried to tell Tasha earlier this week that something is up; I have never known her to be patient when she issues out threats.

Tasha don't give a damn about my current situation. She is too busy focusing on her reality show and trying to find out how one of the Pastor houses was burn down. I haven't heard from Jerrod; he is probably getting high with the money Tasha gave him.

For the past week I have been on pins and needles, walking around town with shorts and tennis shoes on, waiting for a fight. I can't continue living like this. Maybe I am going crazy. I guess it is time to call Asperilla.

The phone rings and the adrenaline run through my body; I can't wait until she answers.

She asks, "Pandora, what is the nature of this call today and are the cops on the line?"

I answer. "I don't need law enforcement to protect me but I'm tired of waiting on you to settle the score, so I'm calling you out anytime, anyplace."

She responds, "Pandora, I find it very funny that you are inviting me to kick your ass. It will come to pass, my dear, but not when you think. You and Serenity talked a lot of shit when I was in jail, only to ignite the fire inside of me. I plotted for months on ways to smash your brain in. Your last words to me were, 'look at your pitiful ass'."

I snap, "Asperilla, you are still pitiful and I don't give a fuck about you beating the charges. If you come over here, be prepared to get your ass stomped."

"Pandora, you are fighting by yourself because Tasha will never have your back," she laughs. "That bitch uses you and treating you like a nasty tampon. You are a piece of shit coming out of her pussy once a month."

I yell, "fuck you, Asperilla! Talk that shit when you are in my face. You have always been a trash talker and the only time you were aggressive is the time we fucked Malakai. You are just another pretty muthafucker who hides behind a piece of dick."

"Yes, we fucked, shared a dick, and you stabbed me in the back over an old flame. I was joking when I called you a retard but you are really slow in the head if you think you have everything under control," Asperilla responds.

"Asperilla, I played your dumbass and I wanted you to rot in jail. But, like Tasha said, you can't do shit without Malakai. No one will ever believe a criminal from Tijuana so we know you are just blowing smoke.

"Allow me to grace you with the honor of why I set your ass up. Serenity created the woman I am today. She was managing the strippers by the time I came on the scene. When I had a chance to sit and talk to her about life, that's when she told me how to escape the club and never return. I came from nothing as well but with her help, I became Pandora with dreams and vision.

"I became jealous when she went to Bible College and dated Carlos. She kept telling me that it was just a scheme but I believe she had feelings for him. I knew the only way to make her upset was to hang with someone twice as pretty as her. You became that person. When the Pastor started cheating with the escorts, Tasha called and asked me whether we were still dating or fucking? I hadn't heard from her in three years but my pussy quivered from her words. Tasha asked me if I had a problem with helping her frame you and kill Malakai? I told her that I would do anything for her and that's when the plan went into effect. Sorry, Charlie!"

"Pandora, I'm so glad you took the time to confess your sins but you should have saved them for Jesus. You are a dead Judas when I see you. Enjoy your last will and testament. I'll see you soon," she admits.

"Asperilla, you better bring it like the Rock!" she yells, slamming down the phone.

I am going to loosen up my evening with a nice glass of wine. I feel better now since I spoke with that little skank.

My phone rings and it better not be Asperilla or I am going to go off. I pick up with the nastiest attitude I could conjure up and say, "Hello!"

Tasha is on the other line saying, "I am coming over to fuck the DNA out of you."

I want to play with my pussy while she is on the phone but I will save all these nuts for her. After fussing with Asperilla, a good dildo and a stiff tongue will be the best distraction a woman needs.

I tell her, "Listen closely to the drips from my pussy hitting the floor like musical notes."

She says, "I will be there later."

I say, "That timing is perfect; I can take a bubble bath and fragrance myself."

I hung up, ran the bath water, light my candles, and play *Lay Down* by Floetry. Slowly, I take off my clothes, layer by layer and I have flashbacks of dancing at the club. I gyrate my hips into the air. I rock to the floor and come up seductively.

I turn the water off and step into the tub to tickle my clit until Tasha arrives. I don't want to cum but I want it so sensitive that when she breathes on it, I squirt instantly.

I am in pure ecstasy, soaking my body. I lift my titties, kiss my nipples, close my eyes, and finger myself like Alicia Keyes on the piano. If I stay in here too long, Tasha will be sucking my leftovers.

I finish my bath, step out the tub, and dry off. I lotion up, spray her favorite perfume and slide my satin Kimono robe on with no panties or bra. I slip into my Louboutin's stilettos, walking towards the mirror and know that it will be a perfect night.

My body is ready for punishment and pleasure. My thoughts are interrupted by the doorbell. *Damn, she is early.* My pussy throbs as I walk towards the door.

I am looking through the peep hole and no one is there so now I turn into survival mode. Grabbing my Glock 19 off the desk, I swung the door open. I don't see anyone so it must have been one of those wild ass kids playing with the bell again. I look down and notice a box sitting on my doorstep. It's a gift-wrapped box with a nice red bow and a note on top saying *Pandora's Box.*

I placed my gun on the box and carried it into the house. I unwrap the gift thirstily with a big ass smile on my face, while tearing through the paper like a wild animal. I open the box and vomit on myself.

I scream, "What the fuck!" while throwing down the box.

I call Tasha but it goes straight to voicemail. I left a message and after the third call, a phone rang and it was not my phone. I hear music playing upstairs and the ringtone is Justin Timberlake's *What Goes Around...Comes Around.* I kick off my stilettos, run upstairs and look at a phone on the bed.

The phone rings again with the same ringtone and this shit is pissing me off. I know Asperilla is behind this shit.

Here I am running around the house paranoid, smelling like vomit. And to make matters worse, I left the damn gun downstairs.

The phone rings again and I throw it as hard as I can against the wall. I leave the bedroom and walk downstairs to see Asperilla sitting on the couch sipping my fucking wine.

"PAYBACK CAN STRIKE YOU WHEN YOU LEAST EXPECT IT. IT'S BETTER TO BE PREPARED THAN TO FACE THE CONSEQUENCES OF BEING CAUGHT OFF-GUARD."

CHAPTER 36

ASPERILLA

I say, "Howdy, Partner! Are you happy to see me? You should put on some clothes because I'm not here to fuck a piece of dead pussy.

"I have been drinking with Jerrod or should I say jack in the box. Wait a minute; time to mourn for my homie," I laugh, while pouring wine on his head.

"I have watched you run like Serena on the tennis court. Did you like the ring tone? I thought it would be perfect for our lovely date. The funniest thing is, when people realize death is coming, they are speechless and shit.

"Pandora, look at your titties hanging; the only good thing about all of this is the coroner will see a freshly shaved pussy. Oh, just so you know, Tasha will not be here anytime soon. She is trying to figure out why her phone isn't working. We had one of our insiders switch the chips so the call can't connect you with Tasha Johnson, Serenity, or that retarded ass First Lady. This is truly a nice gun you have here. Wow, you were going to put one in my head. Just saying the word head makes me laugh.

"I tell you what I'm going to do, since I'm an old school bitch that love to fight. Hold up a second, this wine is delicious; what year is this shit? Anyway, I have been casing your house, listening to your phone calls, and following you around town for the longest. You thought I was just a pretty bitch in heels but as Kevin Hart would say, 'you gon' learn today!'

"You and that bitch are stupid and, for the record, Malakai is not dead. How the hell do you think I am able to pull this shit off? If I was working alone, I would have come in the front door fighting but he is teaching me some art of war type shit.

"Now back to your retarded ass. I am having one of those gladiator moments where we fight until the last person is standing. I have no problem with fighting you naked; hell, we use to fuck and wrestle in the bed anyway."

I sip her glass of wine and point the gun at her so she wouldn't try something stupid. I throw the gun through the window and say, "let's dance, bitch."

I run and jab her with a left hook that causes her to stagger. I jump on her and claw her eyes but she kicks me off her so hard until I hit my head against the wall.

She said, "You are a dumbass. You should have kept that pistol; I'm about to teach you how dirty a street bitch can be."

I get up from the ground and swing but she ducks and punches me in the face. I know she is stronger than me but definitely not smarter. I hit her with an uppercut and a hook to throw her off balance. I bit her ear as hard as I could, worse than Mike Tyson. I am trying to gnaw off her flesh. She punches me in my rib with two sharp blows. I refused to let go of her ear but after the fourth punch, I let go.

She rolls on top of me and chokes me. I gasp for air so I grab her titties and sink my nails deep into them.

"Bitch, let my titties go!" she screams.

I threw her off and clawed her face and followed that by a series of punches. I grab her head and slam it on the floor. I want to see blood burst from the back of her head all the way to her forehead.

She reaches up with a fist full of my hair and slaps the shit out of me. She slides away for a moment. She stands up and tries to run. I kicked her legs and she fell to the floor.

"Bitch! Get over here," I say while punching her face, swinging my blows harder and harder until blood runs from her mouth and nose.

I scream, "You Judas slut, you are going to take this ass beating for betraying me."

I get off her and she turns over and crawls toward the door. I reach into my hair, pull out my razors and slice her arteries. Blood gushes out as I dice through her tendons and she begs me to stop.

I grab one of her knives in the kitchen and she tries to move; time to be the sinister bitch I am known for. I grab Jerrod's head and run his dead face between her nasty cunt.

I laugh, "You bitches deserve to be together. You can die while getting some head, now squirt on that one, bitch."

I grab the knife, crouch down in front of her and say, "This will be over soon so when you get to Hell, tell Satan his daughter says hello."

I wedged the blade into her hollow cavity as a present for Tasha.

I left that slut to die with her eyes wide open to remember how she got to the underworld. I march to the TV, pull out the DVD that Malakai gave me and post a beautiful note on the screen.

I trotted over to Pandora, stomped her face one last time and walk out the door.

My ride is waiting on me and before I can get a chance to sit down, Malakai chuckles, "did you have fun? I was a little worried since you said you only needed ten minutes. I thought Pandora was whooping that ass."

"Pandora put up a little fight but it was worth the kill. We are close to a grand slam and Tasha is next. Why don't you just take the bitch out?" I ask.

He says, "calm down; it has to be done poetically."

"You are always trying to create a fucking memory. You need to remember how to fuck this pussy because killing Pandora has made me super horny," I admit.

CHAPTER 37

TASHA

I am so pissed right now and I will have someone's head for playing with my phone. I only use that phone for business and it has all of my illegal contacts. I only wanted to use Pandora for a publicity stunt at the jail but if the media finds out that we are actually lovers; they will have me on the front page of all the tabloids.

I am driving to her house because I am in desperate need of having my pussy waxed by her tongue. I am flapping this heat between my legs as I approach the last turn to her street.

I need to focus on this Women's Empowerment Conference next month. I plan on taking every simple-minded Christian's money and live out my dreams in Italy.

I pulled into her garage so my rental car wouldn't be seen. I turned the car off, grabbed my purse, and went into the house. The music is playing so I know she's upstairs doing as I requested.

Pandora could have left a light downstairs or something. I turned on the kitchen light and called her name but she didn't answer. I walk into the living room and flip the lamp switch and scream, "what the fuck!"

I see one of the most gruesome things ever. There's a head stuck between Pandora's pussy and her body is lying there with the knife still pressed in her throat. I know this is the work of Asperilla and her friends.

I have a few options left so I move quickly because I am fucked since they found Jerrod's burnt body in Carlos old home. It doesn't take a genius to know it is his head over there.

I turn around and a note is on the TV written, "Dear Punisher, press play."

I hit play on the DVR and see my sexual greed haunting me. I knew all the control and power that I had over Asperilla had come to an end. I watch Malakai fucking the shit out of me in his home; date displayed with the words, *First Lady loves to shout, 'Oh my God!'*

I eject the DVD and call Detective Holiday; he is the only Ace card that I have in my pocket right now.

He says, "Hello."

I say, "John, I am fucked and need you to bail me out. I am at Pandora's house and Jerrod's head is here."

"What do you mean you are there. Are you fucking stupid, Tasha? When you call 911, make sure you are dramatic and horrified. I will take care of everything else when I arrive."

"Thanks, and I promise that after the conference, you will receive everything in full. Since Pandora and Jerrod are out of the way, we have more money to split," I say gratefully.

I put the DVD and note in my purse. Take a short breath to act out my performance. I walk in the kitchen, pull out a knife and slice my arm a few times. This shit hurts like hell but I have to make it seem that I was attacked. I bang my head against the kitchen counter until the blood runs down my face. I picked up the knife, throw it in my purse with everything else in the trunk of my car.

I dial 911. The operator picks up and says, "911, what is your emergency?"

"Help, my friend has been murdered and there is a decapitated head over here. Please send someone now. I am so afraid!" I yell.

"Ma'am is the attacker still in the house?" she questions.

I had to think of the something quick so I respond, "he left after I ran outside screaming."

"Ma'am, are you hurt?" she asks.

"My head is bleeding," I say crying.

"Ma'am, what is your name and address?" she asks sympathetically.

"My name is Tasha Johnson and I am at 2618 Princeton Street. I am standing outside," I respond.

"Ma'am, the officers are on the way," she states.

"Please, don't hang up. I have no idea what to do," I beg.

"Ma'am, I will stay on the phone, so don't panic. Please, don't panic. I will talk to you until the police arrive," she says calmly.

I should have been an actress and it's a great thing Pandora stayed in a lovely neighborhood. I ran out the door and the timing is perfect; I heard the sirens within five minutes. I hung up the phone, crawled through the grass and played the perfect victim. I know Hollywood will call after this performance.

They run up to me and ask, "Is there anyone else in the house?"

I respond, "Yes, but they are dead."

I overheard the officer telling the EMS to make sure I am okay.
They placed me in the ambulance and treated my wounds.

After 15 minutes, Detective Holiday comes over and says,
"Everything will be fine; you are safe now. I will be back after
processing the crime scene."

He is a man of his word because they will never suspect me of
foul play. The saddest part of this night is watching Pandora
carried out in a body bag. I need to get the hell out of this country
quick.

"Mrs. Johnson, I have to go to the station to file this report but
I will stop by the hospital to check on you when I am finished," he
advises.

I tell him, "Thanks for everything," and whispers, "Check the
car."

I am Carlos's wife after all because I can plot ideas just like
him. The only difference is that I am about to become rich in the
process. I will preach the Women's Conference in a body cast if I
have to. Besides, I am a dominant, powerful black woman.

I smile and think of a speech to deliver to the media after I
check out the hospital tomorrow. I need to thank Asperilla again
but she has taken the game to another level with the sex tape. I'll
make sure to plan for that one as well because nothing will stop me
from becoming famous.

CHAPTER 38

MALAKAI

I already know that the DA will hide the news from the media about the First Lady being at Pandora's house. Tasha must have a few crooked politicians by the balls because they are always there to help clean up her mess. I planted some incredible evidence on her so they better be ready for war.

The Women's Conference is less than three days away and I am about to turn her event into the Malakai resurrection.

I sent a text message to the Poetic Heaven Mob Squad, *Good Morning, Squad. I am alive and well but your presence is needed Saturday around 6pm at Truth and Restoration Ministry.*

It didn't take long for the replies with all types of wild ass messages. I will make sure that every artist I know brings the fiyah this weekend.

I call Kryptonite with my other phone. He answers, "You are very lucky that Ayanna told me everything. I should slap your ass for calling me after you faked your own death."

I respond, "I probably deserve the slap but everything is going to be alright. I have been doing a lot of thinking and want to make some changes."

He says, "Just say it, man!"

I confess, "Aight, Asperilla and I are getting married."

I hear him choking as he replies, "Hell naw! What the fuck is wrong with you?"

"Man, I have been with Asperilla for a long time and I could have easily replaced her years ago. I knew what I was getting into the day I met her conniving ass but we endured some beautiful success together. I know deep down that I would rather live my life on the edge with her than play it safe with any other woman," I admit.

He asks, "Can you trust her?"

I respond, "I have never given a woman everything within me and I know it is time. Believe it or not, I trust her with all of my heart."

"Do what you want but make sure to leave my name as the beneficiary for all your properties and other assets," he states.

"On the real, I honor your decision. Plus, if you get married, all the single women at the wedding will need the depression fucked out of them. I will talk to Asperilla personally; she needs to know that if anything happens to you, I will strip her ass naked in front of a firing squad," he says seriously.

"Thanks for being in my corner all these years and our vacation is coming soon," I announce.

He says excitedly, "Let's make it happen next summer. Besides, you need another adventure before eloping with Asperilla."

"Kryptonite, I don't see nothing wrong with that but I gotta run," I say quickly.

"I know you do. I guess you will perform a piece called *Henpecked Poet*," he says, as we hang up.

I walk to my massage recliner, envisioning everything that happened Saturday. I am so close to having my revenge that I can touch it. I know Tasha has watched the sex tape and expects it to be released at the conference but that is too easy.

I reach for the remote, turn on the TV and pray that I can find something to inspire my mind.

I am bored as hell but a big smile comes across my face. I play with man's best friend, Lacy Duvalle's pussy and ass pocket one last time before I throw it away. This shit is perfect for a nut; I never said I'd give up my stimulus package.

This toy has it all, a perfect replica of Lacy's ass and pussy detailed all the way to her contoured painted lips. It even comes with a vibrator for the pulsating feeling. I turn on the vibrator and place it inside the asshole. I pulled down my shorts, lick my fingers and massage my head so I could feel that intense shock when I enter. I pick up the pocket and slide it on my dick. Oh shit! This nut will be a classic. Now all I need is to spit a beautiful poem since I can't turn on the radio.

My mind draws a blank; I've never written anything about pleasuring myself. I say fuck it and start sliding the toy up and down. I am ready to spit with a futuristic perfect flow. I will title this one *Love Thy Self* and I love everything about me.

> *I have no problem pleasuring myself*
> *And I refuse to be ashamed.*
> *I have enough power in my hands*

To call out my own name.

All I have to do is close my eyes

And stroke intimate fantasies

Of wet panties and perfume.

When I want to be romantic,

I'll even light candles

And bring my own sexual ambience into the room.

I love touching myself to some music

Because they say it soothes the savage beast.

Tempos I increase and decrease

Until I am ready to release.

Yes, I do moan when I am in my zone.

I play with my instrument likes it's a trombone

And I'll thrust my inner power from my hipbone.

If I really get into it, then I'll make the bed rock.

Throw my knees up as I begin to buck.

This nut will come and when it does.

Its shoots up my chest,

Once again, these hands are blessed

Regardless of the mess.

While spitting that piece, I slide the pocket pussy up and down like I'm trying to start a fire with two sticks. I rock my hips all into that shit. I should be fucking Asperilla but I need this nut now. I can feel it and the ripples in my abs are shaking from the explosion that is about to come.

I yell, "Oh shit" and shoot through the pocket pussy. This nut is overflowing from the top like a volcano. I exhale and say, "What the fuck! That nut felt great." I should have recorded it so I could watch it in slow motion.

I look down and see that the chair, the pocket pussy, and my chest are cover with cum. I play in it like Play-Doh as I stretch the strings of my nut. I turn around and Asperilla is at the top of the staircase watching.

She yells, "You are a fucking idiot and need to see a damn shrink! All this good pussy right here and you are beating your dick in some fake shit. Tell me this, Malakai; who beats their dick and recites poetry? Never in my life have I seen such craziness. I will give you a '10' on the poetry but quit wasting all my seeds."

I laugh and say, "I am going to take a shower. I will give you a refill in the Jacuzzi this afternoon."

She smiles, "That sounds scrumptious but you need to hurry up before my mouth shuts down like the government."

I say, "You can't do that shit; my soldiers need to find their way to freedom."

She laughs, "That is one of the reasons why I am so in love with you because you are silly but so damn sexy."

"When are you going to let me pick out a tattoo for my perfect ass?" she asks me.

I answer, "Asperilla, you can lick my ass even thumb wrestler in that muthafucker but we are not getting a tattoo."

She says with an attitude, "Fine! But you need to clean up so we can fuck. You still haven't shared your plans with me about Tasha. If I have to go back to jail then I need to get all these orgasms out of me."

I say calmly, "Everything will be fine and I will whisper the plan in your ear as I slow stroke you from behind."

She says, "Now you're talking. I can't wait to enjoy every word."

CHAPTER 39

MALAKAI

"Are you sure you are ready for this because that crooked Detective will be inside to make sure the conference goes as planned?" Asperilla asks.

I answer, "I am expecting that bastard to be her little watchdog but I have a surprise for him too."

I sent out my mob text with the message, *show time will be in 15 minutes.*

I kiss Asperilla and say, "I love you and need you to play your part."

"I was born to be a soldier!" she shouts as she leaves the car.

I watch as she goes into the church and I scroll through the last picture that was taken of me and Love Divine. I kiss the screen and say, "this is my version of Poetic Justice."

I tighten my tie, brush my hair, and step out of my ride. I know Tasha is taping the conference as part of her reality show. I look around the parking lot and see the cars lined up with the media, politicians, and famous preachers.

The church is packed today so I easily walk upstairs and sit in the back of the balcony. The assistant pastor opens up with a prayer and everyone bow their head except me and the music director.

He finishes his prayer and says, "Amen." A lovely elder woman welcomes everyone into the House of the Lord.

She greets a few by names and speaks, "this conference is about restoring women's confidence across the globe. When God created us, he knew that man needed a help meet and a soul mate. This evening all I ask is that we reunite souls back to the Maker."

She shouts, "Glory to God," and you could hear the whole church echo it back like thunder. "I will turn things over to the woman of the hour, the voice of the future, one of the strongest and exquisite women of faith. Allow me to introduce Evangelist Tasha Johnson."

Everyone stands to their feet, clapping and shouting as she walks to the stage. She is really good at being a scammer. I would have never imagined this woman could plot a murder and take money from people.

I am not sure if I am on a mission for God or myself but I know these people work too hard to have their dreams stolen by her lies.

"I know you are ready for a life changing experience and ready to walk into your destiny. No, we have been waiting too long; it's time to run into your destiny; we have endured and trained for this moment all of our lives. I need some Christians that are ready, turn around, hi-five your neighbor and say run! I will turn it over to the music director for a beautiful selection," she concludes.

The audience stands as he tells the church it is time to praise and enter into the realm of worship.

He claps his hand and the pianist plays the tune of *Nobody Greater* and that song always makes me freeze and rejoice. I sing the chorus,

Searched all over... couldn't find nobody

I looked high and low... still couldn't find nobody
Nobody greater... nobody greater no...
Nobody greater than you.

It's amazing the way God uses music to soothe a hurting soul.

The music plays, choir hum and a woman come down the aisle.

She stands by the stage and praise dances gracefully. Tasha has a confused look but I know she won't stop it because this will make her look famous and the cameras are rolling.

The dancer grabs a guy from the front row and he dances alongside her. They skip down the aisle spinning and turning for God. They make their way to the stage with twenty more dancers.

They are forming a formation and the music director waves his hand stopping the crowd from singing. He looks at me and I know it is time to wipe the smile off of Tasha's face.

The choir sings Shirley Caesar's *Satan, We're Gonna' Tear Your Kingdom Down*. The first poet spits spoken word while the choir and church hum along.

I am watching as the poets come down the aisle and deliver some of the most gifted pieces imaginable and they love every minute of it.

I couldn't just come into the House of the Lord without giving honor to the creator so I walked downstairs. I can hear their voices filling the empty souls in the room as they poured their heart out with small testimonials, life challenges, and becoming victorious over their destinies.

I am waiting for the last poet to spit his piece and they sing cadence in one angelic voice.

I step through the aisle and grab Asperilla by the hand as if we were going to the altar to get married and say,

Satan I am about to tear your kingdom down.
Your trickery and lies are to be exposed
And with these flows I come to save a soul.
This is my poetic gift from God
Who uses my tongue as a scroll
To unleash heat
When I have to tear the head off the beast.
I walk these streets like a disciple alone or with twelve.
I dwell in hell's kitchen.
I have been ordained and commissioned
To speak words to make the world listen.
Allow me to flip these words into your soul so acrobatic
I can help you solve your life equations,
The answer lies with the Greatest Mathematic.
Whom never needs you to use big numbers
But wants you to see
One plus two equals the Trinity.
This is how you walk into your destiny.
You leave behind jealousy.
God wants to perform a vasectomy
Sterilize your mind that is so confine and out of line.

Even though He is everywhere,
You keep pushing Him behind
Then you wonder why you are still walking blind.
My destiny is Hi-story,
I stand before You and offer my body
As a living sacrifice
Sometimes we can roll the dice
And God will allow you to crap out
Before He pulls you out.

The choir continues humming; that must have been part of God's plan to reach me one last time because that wasn't the piece I was going to spit. Asperilla looks at me all silly eyed and confused and whispers, "What the hell you are doing?"

I nod to the musician that I am done; the church stands and shouts, "Spoken Word, Spoken Word, and Spoken Word."

Tasha walks to the stage and says, "I told you that God is omnipotence. I am blessed to have so many beautiful and talented artists with us. Give God the praise for He is worthy in this place tonight."

The audience clap and wave their hands in appreciation of the mob's ministry.

The mob disperses throughout the church and the music director plays again as I kiss my future wife's hand and we walk out.

The weather is perfect outside; she looks at me and asks, "Do you mean that we took out Jerrod and Pandora for nothing?"

I smile and answer, "Something happened when I opened my mouth. I was going to expose her but I guess God touched my soul."

"Well, God need to touch mine because I want that bitch dead but if that's how you feel then I am going to follow your lead, Malakai," she says.

The mob shows love and says, "We have never mobbed a church before and it will be exciting to be on the news for something positive this time. Thanks for the opportunity and we will be at Poetic Heaven next weekend."

I tell them, "I can't wait and you know the mic will be on fire for all of you. Thanks again for the favor and I'll make sure the whole bar and food is free when ya'll come."

I watch as they get into their cars and leave.

Asperilla asks, "Well, since you are changing, does that mean we are shutting down the business?"

I responds, "I am committed to one woman, forgiving my enemies, but my changes are coming one day at a time."

"You have made me so proud of you today and when we get home tonight, I am going to demonstrate it in so many ways. By the way, I threw away all of your pockets pussies," she says with a smile.

"Woman you gonna mess around and be engaged to your damn self," I say as I laugh and press my lips against hers.

Our intimate moment was broken by the great Detective Holiday as he says, "Both of you are a pain in my ass. Malakai, you should have stayed a corpse. Y'all, think you have everyone fooled but Tasha texted me during the service and she wants the sex tapes."

"What the hell are you talking about?" I ask.

"Don't fucking play with me, Malakai!" he yells.

"Look, Detective. I don't know anything about a sex tape," I say calmly.

"Well, that's fine. Maybe jail will change your mind until you can produce it," he responds.

I snap, "I don't like your dirty ass and I know you have been cleaning up her mess for a long time. You are not the only one with friends at the station."

"So, are you threatening me right now, nigga? Because I can handcuff and beat you to death in an alley. I'll frisk your woman. I can see my hands running up and down her legs. Matter of fact, church or no church, there is a restraining order against her and Tasha want that ass in jail right now. I will be touching that sweet pussy after all. I hope that's not a problem if I play cops and robbers with your bitch," he laughs.

"Asperilla is not going anywhere," I say as I crack the biggest smile. "Sometimes it's better to take a person's apology and run."

Asperilla pulls out the tape recorder so his retarded ass can hear all the shit he was talking.

"I can't prove all the shit you have done in the past but I do have that special phone call conversation between you and Tasha that night Pandora was murdered. I believe you were the one who staged the whole set, tampered with evidence, and took a bribe. That means jail time; you know what they do to crooked cops behind prison walls."

"Nigga, I'll kill your ass," he says as he reaches for his gun. I look over to see a sexy white cop reminding me of Calleigh Duquesne off CSI Miami. She walks over and smiles, "Malakai, I knew this would have worked out to benefit us both. Thanks for your cooperation but we will take it from here. Detective, you are under arrest. Please hand over your gun and badge because you aren't worthy of being a cop."

They handcuff him and throw him in the back seat.

"Don't drop the soap unless you want to become the master of deep throating," I say with a sly grin.

"Have you two fucked before because she is a little too damn friendly? I would hate to be in the back seat with Detective Holiday for fucking her up," Asperilla says.

"How you think I was able to get that information off of their phone. They have been trying to bring him down for a long time. Back in my whoring days, I fucked her so good that she offered me a job. Who would have ever imagined the outcome when I found out that him and Tasha were working together?"

I feel the sting from her slap, not once but twice, and I ask, "What the fuck that was for?"

She replies, "That's for leaving me in jail knowing you had an inside source to get me out earlier."

Rubbing my jaw and I say, "Damn. I thought we were even when you bit my dick?"

"Nah, that was extra. Plus, I can never get upset over your past; the present and future will get your balls cut off and shoved in your mouth if you cheat on me. Now what are we going to do about Tasha since she will be in jail," she smiles and speaks.

I tell her, "I always have a Plan B but Tasha doesn't deserve to live. She's not going to jail today." I grab her hand, walk to the church, and attend the fireworks that will light up the whole room.

"NOT EVERYONE NEEDS TO KNOW YOUR PLANS, SO IT'S WISE TO KEEP SOME THINGS TO YOURSELF. A TRUE BOSS ALWAYS HAS A BACKUP PLAN."

CHAPTER 40
MALAKAI

We walked into the building just in time because she is about to preach her sermon.

I look towards the ceiling and say, "God, you know I tried; we will have to talk about this one later."

I say to Asperilla, "We are about to make history in a few minutes."

She smiles because she knows I am planning something big. I am extra excited since I paid some guys in the media room to broadcast Tasha's business all over the conference.

I watch as she walks toward the stage like the Queen of England, as if everyone should bow and worship her. I keep my composure as she sets up. She always valued herself as a Proverb 31 type woman and I know she will speak from it.

As she speaks, the words are displayed on the screen for the church to follow. I wait until she reaches that dominant verse; she reads the words, "speaks with wisdom and faithful instruction is on her tongue."

The instruction on her tongue line is the cue for the media to rewind it a few times.

She says while glancing, "Well church I guess the screen loves to recite faithful instructions is on her tongue. I believe God want us, as His people, to have instructions upon our tongue."

I text my friend in the media room and he texts back to tell me everything is live and they will leave the video playing and lock the room.

She continues talking and the words on the screen display, *Tasha loves to praise when her legs are raised.* The video plays it in slow motion for the entire church to see how high she raises her legs. She had her toes touching the back of the headboard as I was drilling her out.

Only in America, members pull out their phones to record the video. I guess this plan worked out for the best because this will be seen all over World Star Hip Hop before the conference ends.

"Turn that off!" Tasha screams.

She dashes off the stage with the other members of the pulpit. The sounds from the video became louder with her favorite verse flashing all over the screen.

"I believe this is some of your best poetry in motion. I told you before that you should have been a poetic porn star or something," says Asperilla.

I am watching the commotion as people are running out of the building with shame. Her investors are pissed because they poured a lot of their money into her ministry.

Tasha finally gets into the media room to stop the video but the aftermath has been built in front of her eyes. She comes back to the stage to calm everyone down but it was useless; majority of them walked past her shaking their heads in disbelief.

The best part about today is the conference is still being filmed throughout this whole evening. We are making reality TV and she will become famous for her mouth after all.

She looks over at us and says, "Don't think this is over. I promise you all will pay for what you have done." Then she screams, "I have been framed and the real criminals are standing before us."

I know it is impossible to touch her with her entourage standing so close but I will wait patiently for the right opportunity. The Bay 9 News is always the first on the scene; rushing through the doors to get a comment from the infamous Tasha Johnson.

She sees them heading in her direction with the police. Her team escorts her to the rear of the building.

I tell Asperilla, "let's go home, there is nothing more to see," as we start walking out of the door.

I received a text from a good friend telling me the plan worked perfectly and the gift will be delivered by tomorrow night.

I start the car and ask Asperilla, "How does Cuba sound for a mini vacation?"

She answers, "I would love to get out of Florida for a minute; this has been one crazy ass year."

"Awesome, we will leave tomorrow," I say and plant a wet kiss on her lips.

We drove home and for the first time I am really happy; feels wonderful to relax without any drama.

I will work on changing the club's name to Divine Love in honor of her legacy. I know she would have been truly proud of the changes I have made in my life.

We walk into the door and I must say it has been one hell of a day since the sex monster says, "I want to take a shower and go to bed."

I tell her, "get undress but skip the shower."

She turns and asks, "What are you talking about?"

I answer, "Meet me in the whirlpool in 15 minutes. I want to wash you while reading you poetry tonight."

She says blushing, "you haven't done anything like that for me in ages."

I kiss her lips and say, "sometimes when you are on top of the world, you have to remember who helped you get there, so hurry up."

I prepared the water and candles for her arrival. She walks in with nothing on and I know that she is the woman that I can love forever.

I grab her favorite body wash and use my hands to rub it all over her. Her moans give me the key to let me know that she is enjoying every touch.

I squeeze the water down her chest and she says, "You need to stop because we are not fucking tonight."

I smile and say, "I am in complete harmony with you right now and I can wait."

She lays back and says, "I am ready to hear your beautiful poetry."

She closes her eyes; I soak and rinse her body over and over again.

I parted my lips so my words could seep out and enter into her soul.

Thoughts are created in the mind,
Perceived through your five senses.
I can whisper I love you when I'm not around you.
I can feel your legs shake before you masturbate.
I can imagine kissing you and when you lick your lips,
I can vision your body dripping in cold sweat.
I'm trying to stimulate all of your nerves
Until you just forget.
Forget your name, your birth, and your life.
I want to invade your mind
Until you climax with success;
Seduce your cerebrum
Until I dive under your brain stem.
I'm thinking of new ways to make you happy
Beyond the next decade.
My thoughts will march through your organic structure
Like a Macy's Day parade.
My mental stimulation packs explosion like a grenade.
I shall invade and cater to your dreams

Like a merry maid.

I don't want to just touch you.

I want to use this poetic tongue

To blow right through you.

Blow a hole in your soul like ladies panty hose

On Sunday, all day.

Thinking of you is my foreplay.

Asperilla, I want my thoughts to work on you hard

And long like an essay.

Allow me to enter your mental temple.

Whatever you request, I will obey.

Malakai is back;

Tell your distractions to get the hell out of my way.

I have returned with so much hunger.

I want my words to be so deep

Until they place you in a coma.

Then I'll whisper rise up

And my aura will be the aroma

That stimulates your nerves to jump out of your seat.

I'm ready to make you speak a new language

From Japanese to Portuguese.

I promise my mental stimulation

Will bring you to your knees.

I want to taste your dreams, make love to your vision.

Now stop with the hesitation

And let me give you this mental stimulation.

Asperilla opens her eyes and says, "after all of that, you still not getting any pussy, no head and definitely no ass. I will give you a kiss for effort."

I laugh and say, "I will be fine tonight and you can sleep in peace."

I continue giving her a soothing bath experience. I wash every part of her clean, dry her off, blow on her toes for fun, and moisturize her body with her favorite lotion.

I carried her to the bedroom and lay her on the sheets. We talk about our future and in less than ten minutes, she is asleep.

Now it is time for me to jump in the shower. I wash, dry off, walk out with no clothes and head straight to the window. I love looking at the world the way God intended it to be, buck naked and free. I smile and try to touch the moon and stars like a little kid who has dreams of flying across the sky.

We have been shopping all day and Asperilla wants to go dancing at *El Delirio Habanero*.

I ask, "I will take you tomorrow, if it's okay?"

"Why in the hell did you bring me to Cuba and not take me dancing? I could have stayed in Tampa to shop and gone to *Hyde Park Café*!" she yells.

I tell her, "I am always full of surprises. Just trust me on this one."

"Whatever! You better make sure that it is something that I will love," she says while twirling her hair.

I opened her car door and ask her to get in so I can take her somewhere special.

We travel down the road until we arrive at a gated home. "This house is huge, Papi. Who lives here?" she asks.

"A few old friends and one special person" I respond, as her eyes becomes wider as we pull to the front.

Edmundo meets and greets me with the biggest hug he could. "Welcome to Cuba. Asperilla, my dear, please allow me to kiss your hands. I will never wash my lips again. Leave your bags, my staff will take care of them," Edmundo says while opening the door.

We walk into the house and down a long hall. He leads us to his famous secret room and opens the door. Inside is a woman blindfolded, gagged, and tied for our pleasure.

He has prepared everything for us so we can take our time. He said he would see us upstairs for dinner later on and he walk out and close the door behind him.

"Malakai, is that who I think it is? How in the hell did you get her here?"

I respond, "Yep! That's Tasha Johnson, in the flesh. If she wasn't so greedy and deceitful, she probably would have made it out of the church. I had a team set up outside to grab her during the distraction and bring her here."

Asperilla walks over, loosens the blindfold, and removes the gag ball from her mouth and says, "Good evening, Punisher; or should I say Serenity or First Lady. The time has come and even though I promise to have an orgasm over your death, I will suck this one back in."

I march over and say to Tasha, "Your husband was a dirty ass preacher and he had plenty of ladies but he crossed the lines when he had one of my girls beaten. I told him that I would go to great lengths to protect my ladies but you are about to find out what I am capable of when you kill one of my poetic friends."

"I believe it is time to baptize Tasha with her lies because her flesh is rotten and deserves to be eaten alive," I tell Asperilla.

Tasha begs and says, "ya'll don't have to do this. I will leave Florida and never return," while kneeling and praying for us not to do the unthinkable.

I look down and say, "You had your chance yesterday but you wanted to send your little crooked cop to threaten our lives over a sex tape. I was willing to walk out of church and forgive you but just like your husband, you all have fucked with the wrong poet. Besides, you were going to jail anyway, so consider this a favor."

She looks up and say, "wait Malakai, I know there is still some good in your heart."

I utter, "yes, and there was good in Love Divine's heart before her throat was slashed."

Asperilla pulls out her blades and says, "teatime is over, Bitch." She slices Tasha arms so damn quick that I didn't see her put the blades back into her pocket.

Tasha screams louder and louder. Asperilla says, "Malakai, thank you for the best present ever. I know you are the poet but I am about to show you what I can do on a stage. I saw the movie *300* last week and this is the perfect scene to act out.

"Earth and Water, well Tasha, you will find plenty of those down there. You brought crowns and heads of conquered Kings to my city steps. You insulted me as a Queen. You threatened my people with slavery and death. Oh, I chose my words carefully, Tasha. Perhaps you should have done the same," speaking with fire in her voice.

Tasha says, "Your bitch is crazy and you need to control her."

Asperilla says, "This is not madness. This is Sparta!!!"

She kicks Tasha ass into the pool with hungry sharks as they rip into her flesh instantly. They are gnawing their teeth into her fucked up soul. I see one bite out her eyeball. They are feasting on her like Thanksgiving dinner, tearing the skin and meat from her limbs.

I can tell that Asperilla enjoys watching the terror before her eyes.

She whispers to me, "I will be busting a few nuts tonight, because that has made me so fucking horny."

She turns around and does her favorite Dorothy's heel clap and says, "there is no place like home and I am ready to go."

I grab her by the hand and say, "let's go upstairs to meet Edmundo and his family."

We look back one last time and say, "Exit Stage Left. End piece!"

ABOUT THE AUTHOR

Flenardo is an ordinary man that decided to manifest his dreams into reality with a creative stroke of imaginative superpowers. His passion to do the unthinkable will always be his adrenaline rush toward the next adventures. He can be reached at www.freknardo.com